On the Train to My Village
a novel

Autumn Bird
selected poems

Akhtar Naraghi

Library and Archives Canada Cataloguing in Publication

Naraghi, Akhtar
On the train to my village; &, Autumn bird :
new fiction and selected poems / Akhtar Naraghi.

ISBN 978-1-897336-77-9

I. Title. II. Title: Autumn bird.

PS8577.A665O58 2011 C813'.54 C2011-904996-1

Published in Canada by Price-Patterson Ltd.
Canadian Publishers
Montreal, Canada

Book layout & design: Ted Sancton/Studio Melrose

Cover photo © Kurt Stricker, 2009.

Contents

On the Train to My Village

I lifted my head when the train sounded its whistle, and from my seat I peered through the dusty window of the compartment. The sun was pausing to paint the sky mystically red before sinking below the horizon. I was going back to the Gaspé village where I was born and raised. Suddenly I felt terribly lonesome. I got up and walked to the dining car, and asked for a cup of tea. As I waited for it I put my tired head down on the table, and thoughts of the Gaspé drifted into my mind.

*   *   *

"Lisa!"

I heard my mother's voice cry from the open window of the kitchen. "Lisa, where are you! What are you doing?"

"I'm here, Mamma! I'm taking the sheets off the clothesline. You told me to."

"Hurry! Go get your Aunt Monique! Tell her I'm in labour!"

She disappeared from the window. I dropped what I had in my hands and ran as fast I could to my aunt's house.

Aunt Monique was cooking supper when I rushed into the kitchen. "Auntie, please hurry! Mamma's going to have her baby, please come with me!"

She looked at me, alarmed. "Oh, my God – the baby's premature!" Hurriedly she switched off the stove and pulled off her apron. Without another word she took my

5

hand, and we dashed out as if the house were in flames.

On our way to my home, Aunt Monique knocked frantically on doors to ask for help. "Marie-Josée's in early labour!" Three women joined us, and we all raced to the house. When we got halfway, Aunt Monique said, "The rest of you go on. I'll get the midwife."

At the house the three women rushed upstairs to help my mother, but one came back down immediately and asked me to wait with my two little sisters outside.

I took the hands of Nicole and Carole, and nervously we went out to the veranda. As we stepped out the door, Aunt Monique and the midwife rushed past us. My sisters and I sat down, facing the sea, but we would fretfully keep turning our heads to see what was going on inside the house.

The women went up and down the stairs, carrying sheets, towels and boiling water. We could hear the voice of our mother crying for help. As we watched the women inside, Carole gripped my hand tightly.

"Lisa!" she cried. "Do you know why Mamma is screaming?"

"She's going to have a baby. It must hurt a lot."

"I don't want the baby hurting my mamma! I'm going upstairs to help her!" She let go of my hand and headed towards the door. I stopped her and said gently, "You can't help Mamma, you're six years old. You don't understand these things."

Nicole looked at me and said impatiently, "Well I'm *eight* years old, and *do* understand. Tell me: why is Mamma really screaming?"

"Because the baby's coming out of her, and it's painful."

"How is the baby coming out?" the younger one asked.

"I don't know. Both of you leave me alone," I said irritably, trying to concentrate on the sound of my mother's voice.

Abruptly, after all the screaming and cries for help, there was silence. I felt elated. "I think the baby's come out of Mamma!" I said to my sisters.

The sun was sinking and in the distance a train was sounding its whistle when Aunt Monique finally rushed from the house. Her eyes were wide with panic. "Lisa, hurry! Your Mamma wants to see you. But be careful, don't say anything to upset her!" I ran upstairs.

My mother lay on the bed, her face whiter than the walls. Her eyes were barely open and her wet hair was spread all over the pillow. Everything around her was red. The sheets, the towels, the bed itself: they were all soaked in her blood. Seeing so much blood made me sick to my stomach; I felt stabbings of pain in my heart. For a moment I froze, but Aunt Monique kept moving me towards Mamma's bed. As I got closer, I saw a tiny purple baby's face poking from a white towel on the night table. "Don't look at him, he's dead," Aunt Monique said. "Look at your mother; she wants to talk to you."

I knelt down beside my mother's bed and took her hand. It was so cold it made me shiver. "Mamma, it's me," I said softly. "It's Lisa. You asked for me; here I am." I didn't know what else to say.

With great effort my mother opened her eyes, She looked at me and said with a feeble voice, "Listen to me, dear. I don't have much longer. You have to promise me that you'll look after yourself, and also your sisters and your papa."

She closed her eyes, and struggling for breath, continued, "I know you can do it. I know you're a strong and brave girl. You're eleven years old, but you're more mature than your age. I *know* you can do it. You have to promise me you'll look after everyone."

Still holding her hand I said, "Mamma, you'll be okay. I know you'll be okay. I'll pray for you. But if you want me to promise you, I'll promise."

"Good girl," she breathed. "Now go and be with your sisters. Never forget that you're a brave girl and that I'm very proud of you," she managed, and tried to open her eyes again, but couldn't. She was semiconscious when I left the room and ran down the stairs.

"Come with me!" I told my two sisters roughly. "Both of you come with me!" I took their hands and ran down behind the house near our potato field. I asked Nicole and Carole to kneel down with me, join hands, look at the sky and repeat after me: "Dear God, please help Mamma. Please, *please* don't take Mamma away from us."

Nicole and Carole began to bombard me with questions about our mother. I didn't know what to say. Fear was making my mouth dry and my head pound. In order to keep myself and my sisters busy I said, "Let's go pick some green beans for supper," and took their hands again.

"I don't want to pick green beans. I want to know what's wrong with Mamma," Nicole insisted, pulling her hand away.

Angrily I snapped, "Okay! If you really want to know, Mamma is bleeding to death!"

"Why?" she said, panicking.

"Because of the baby."

"I don't know why Mamma has to have so many babies! Who wants Mamma to have more babies?"

"It's God's commandment: women must be pregnant all the time and keep having babies."

"I don't believe it! You're lying!"

"Mamma told me herself."

"But I don't believe God wants Mamma to bleed to death!"

"I don't believe it either," I said.

Carole came and whispered in my ear. "Lisa, listen! I know who wants Mamma to have more babies."

"Who?"

"Papa's the one who wants to have more babies. One day he told me he wants three brothers for us."

"Okay, that's enough!" I said. "Let's kneel down and pray again. I'm just so frightened. I saw Mamma's blood all over the place."

"Where's the baby?" Carole asked.

"He's dead," I answered flatly.

"Oh no. Was he a boy? Oh no, my baby brother is dead!"

"Who cares about your baby brother," I answered angrily. "Mamma is bleeding to death."

Suddenly I heard Aunt Monique bawling, "We have to get her to town, to the hospital!" And another woman's voice answered loudly, "It's too late! I said it's too late!"

Aunt Monique shrieked, "No! No! She can't die. You're a midwife, why can't you do something?" And the woman answered, "She's lost too much blood, there was nothing I could do. Don't you see: she's *dead*."

I had been standing motionless, listening to their argument. I began to tremble. I couldn't believe my mother was dead. All of a sudden I felt lonely and disoriented. The world had become a foreign place to me; I felt I'd been erased from it. With no concern that it was getting dark, I ran past the potato field and into the woods, trying to get the smell of death off myself. I could hear Nicole and Carole shouting: "Lisa! Lisa! Where are you going? It's getting dark! You'll get lost in the woods!" But I ran fast, and was soon out of their sight.

*   *   *

"Are you okay?" A man patted me on the shoulder. "You've had your head on the table forever, and haven't touched your tea." I looked up at him through teary eyes. "Oh, yes!" I said. "Thank you, I'm fine."

There was compassion in his eyes. "Do you mind if I join you?"

"Please do," I said, trying to be polite. But I wasn't in any mood to carry on a conversation, and the man noticed.

"Am I disturbing you? Would you rather I left?"

"Oh, no," I said, despite myself. "Please don't go."

He said, "My name is Noel."

"And I'm Lisa," I replied. "Nice to meet you."

I shook his hand and stole a glimpse at his face. He was in his mid-thirties with ocean-blue eyes and sandy hair that he wore rather long. He had a charming face and a pleasant smile. For a moment he looked at me and I looked at him, and there was silence between us.

"You have a name given to a lot of Indians in this part of the world," I said, "but there's nothing Native about the way you look."

"You're right. My parents are Irish and I was born in the Gaspé. My name comes from something that happened with my mother when she was a teenager. What about you?" he asked gently.

"I was born in the Gaspé region too, to a French-Canadian mother and an Irish father."

"Well then we both have Irish blood. Maybe we're related!"

"Maybe. Who knows?"

"I'm on my way to the Gaspé now. Are you headed there too?"

"Yes, but it's such a distance from Montreal."

"It *is* really a long trip," he said. He glanced out the window, then turned back to me with his charming smile. "You know, I believe it's just about dinnertime. Would you care to join me?"

"Of course. I'd be happy to."

We found a table away from the other diners. "I love eating on a train," Noel said. "I find the food has a different taste."

"How do you mean?"

"Well, I don't mean the taste of food on a train is different. I meant eating in the dining car on a train gives you a different feeling than in other places. There's a sense of freedom: belonging nowhere, and yet belonging everywhere. I love to eat when the train's moving fast. I love to hear its whistle blow."

"I feel the same way. And I have to add, travel by train is so much better than by plane. On a plane you vanish into the void. You feel you're flying over something, yet there's nothingness. But on a train you feel you belong to the land."

"You know," he said with a childlike excitement, "I'm so glad we agree with each other! Why don't you order for us." I told him whatever he chose to eat was fine with me too.

As we were sharing a glass of wine and waiting for our meal, Noel said, "You haven't asked me anything about my life."

I smiled. "I don't believe it's polite to ask people a lot of questions about their lives. If they want to talk, they will. Of course I'd like to hear about you and your work."

"I'm an artist."

"Well, that's something interesting. What kind of art do you do?"

"I paint."

"What sorts of things do you paint?"

"Most of the time I paint nature, and I do oils. But sometimes I do portraits too."

He looked at me closely. "I have to say, you have a wonderful face for drawing. You have lovely deep, sad amber eyes, full lips, a long neck, thick chestnut hair, splendid colour in your cheeks – everything's perfect for drawing. I'd love to do your portrait one day."

I blushed. "Thank you for the compliment," I said, "but I think you need glasses."

Noel seemed taken aback. "I was joking," I assured him. "I really appreciate the lovely compliment. I'm flattered."

"Everything I said is true, and I'm sure many people have told you how beautiful you are."

"Never mind me. Tell me a little about your background."

He picked up his glass of wine and finished what was left. "My great-grandfather was a famous painter in Ireland. We have a stunning piece of his work in our home. It's a scene of an Irish village. You have to see it, I can't do it justice for you."

"Can you at least tell me a little about the painting, so maybe I can picture it in my mind?"

"You see, although the picture is a view of a village, it looks as if it's about all of Ireland, and the greenness of the whole land. It's a small frame, yet it holds so many different greens, and it captures the mystical feeling of the land. The piece is one of Great-grandfather's finest works, and my grandmother gave it to my mother when she got married. She asked my mother to keep the painting in the family.

"As a young boy I was fascinated by the picture, and I would sit for hours and hours looking at it without getting tired of it. I would ask my mother questions about the land and the painter and she would patiently answer all of them. The more I looked at the painting the more I wanted to become a painter, and my mother encouraged me a lot. She's a wonderful soul."

As he talked, the waiter brought our food and refilled our glasses. For a few minutes we paid attention to our meal. Then I said, "Tell me about your mother. The way you talk about her, I'd really like to know more. But eat first."

"Don't worry about my food. If you really want to know about my mother, first I have to tell you something about her love life."

"I'm all ears," I said.

Noel gazed down into his glass for a moment, took a sip of wine and began to talk.

"When my mother was fifteen and living with her parents in Douglastown, in the Gaspé, she took a job in a small gift shop. There was an Indian boy by the name of Noel working in the shop too. After a few weeks of working together, my mother and Noel fell madly in love."

"Oh!" I interrupted. "So that's what you meant about your mother choosing the name Noel for you."

"Yes. Noel was the love of her life."

"So what happened?"

Noel looked at me and smiled. "It *is* a good feeling to

eat in the dining car of a train, isn't it – especially when someone tells you a love story at the same time."

"Yes," I agreed. "It's always good to hear a love story. 'There's only one love story, yet every time you hear it it's unique in its own way.' I hope this one's not a very sad one, though."

"Then maybe it's better I stop there."

"No, no! Go ahead and tell me more. But as much as I want to hear it, I don't want your food to get cold. Let's leave the love story of your mother for after our dinner."

When dinner was over, Noel fell into a silence that grew long enough to make me wonder; then he drank the rest of the wine in his glass.

"One day the Indian boy Noel didn't show up at the shop, and as my mother stood there worrying about what might have happened to him, a tall solidly built man with a heavy Indian way of walking came into the store. He stood straight, like a soldier, looked at my mother and said, 'Are you the Margaret that my son is in love with?' And my mother, not one to be intimidated, answered firmly, 'Yes, I'm the Margaret who's in love with your son.'

"'You'd better forget about Noel,' the man said coldly. 'I don't want any foreigner getting involved with my son. We have to marry among ourselves. We don't want mixed blood.'

"My mother answered him back sharply. 'The blood has been mixed since Europeans first got here. Now when it comes to me, you don't want me to be with your son.'

"'If we don't like foreigners, we have our reasons.'

"'And those would be?'

"'You are white, and we don't forget what you have done to us.'

"'I didn't do anything to you and your people. I just love your son.'

"'He will not see you anymore.'

"'And what will happen if he does?'

"'He knows he will be cursed for the rest of his life,' Noel's father said, 'and he will be a member of us no longer.' And with that he left the shop without waiting for my mother to respond. It was such a brief conversation that my poor mother didn't really have time to comprehend. From that day on there was no trace of Noel. You can picture the rest of the story. My mother was devastated and his parents ended up moving to another county. But to this day my mother has not forgotten Noel. After all these years of being married to my father, she still talks about him. Once I asked her why she loved Noel so much. She said that he was mysterious, attractive, generous, and so kind. He was different from other boys."

"What about your father?" I asked.

Noel replied firmly, "My parents love each other dearly, and my father understands that my mother is still searching for Noel and would like to see him again."

"Do you blame Noel's father?"

"I don't know."

"Are you going to the Gaspé to find Noel?"

"Noel is sitting in front of you."

"I mean the Indian one."

"Who knows? No, I'm joking; I'm going to the Gaspé to paint. I don't have to tell you how spectacular the scenery is."

I was tired and it was quite late; I felt I was falling asleep in my chair. Looking at Noel I said, "It would probably be a good idea to rest for a few hours, and then come back to have some coffee and talk again." A smile crossed Noel's face, but I could tell that deep down he didn't want me to leave. Still he said, "That's probably a good idea," and we both left the dining car.

I sank into my seat and closed my eyes to sleep, but couldn't. I gazed out; there was nothing except the darkness of the night, which frightened me: it reminded me of the night my mother passed away.

*   *   *

"Lisa, Lisa, why are you running away!" I could hear Nicole's screaming and Carole's whimpering, but I kept running through the woods as if an avalanche were chasing me. I was running away from the smell of death, but as fast as I was running, I realized the more I moved away from the death of my mother the closer I came to it. I ran, screaming and calling out, "Mother, come back, don't leave me alone! I need you! We *all* need you!"

Suddenly the heavy dangling branch of a tree knocked me to the ground. Blood ran down my face, and the pain was unbearable. I passed out.

"Lisa! Lisa, where are you?" I tried to force my eyes open, but I could only open the left one a little, and barely made out a few men I knew from the village with their lanterns walking quickly through the woods, searching for me and calling my name. I heard my Uncle Fred's voice shouting, "Lisa, my girl, where are you? Don't be scared! Tell me where you are. We'll find you. Stay wherever you are. We'll find you!" But I was semi-conscious and didn't have the strength to shout and tell him where I was.

"Here she is!" I finally heard Uncle Fred call out. "Poor little thing." He lifted me up. The men brought their lanterns close and looked down at me. "Oh, God. Look at the blood on her face. Look at her eyes." One of the men took me from my uncle and carried me in his arms to our home. After that I remember nothing until I heard the voices of Carole and Nicole.

"Lisa, we love you, you'll be okay!" I could still hardly open my right eye; I felt the thickness of bandages on my face. "Oh, Carole!" Nicole said excitedly. "Did you see: she opened her eyes!" They sat on the edge of the bed and held my hands "That's good. I can give her something to eat now," Carole said, and after putting two pillows under my head began to feed me spoonful after spoonful of chicken soup. It took a long time for me to finish. But I got a little bit of my strength back, and managed to ask what had happened to me that made me so sick. Nicole told me that after they brought me home, for a few days I was so ill I didn't even know where I was. Then she said, "But don't worry, we'll look after you now." And I began to weep, quietly but from deep within.

For days more I lay in bed with fever and terrible pain. I didn't know when my father came back from his job on the fishing boat. I had no idea when my mother was buried. I had little awareness of what was going on around me. I knew that my two little sisters and Aunt Monique were with me most of the time, and that they fed me, but not a lot more.

I was doing a little bit better, when one day I heard my father's sad voice. "How's my little girl doing?" he said as he entered the room. I tried to get out of bed, but he came towards me and took me in his arms. "Oh, Papa, you know Mamma is gone!" I said, choking on my tears.

"I know, and it was my fault. I'm the one who wanted to have more children."

"Don't say that, Papa! Please don't say that!"

"Your mamma was so young and so beautiful. She was an angel." He tried hard not to sob in front of me. Aunt Monique, who had followed my father in, stated evenly, "It was God's will. He knows best." I was going to say something, when Nicole interjected, "Papa, Lisa ate all her soup. I fed her really well!" Carole also jumped into the conversation. "*I* helped her too!"

My father looked at my sisters. "With your mamma gone, you have to look after each other now. We all have to look after each other." I saw how bleak he looked, and how vacant his eyes were, how all his natural exuberance had drained away. I was worried; for a moment I forgot my own pain. He hugged me again and stroked my arm. "My dear, I came up to see you many times, but you were always asleep. I'm right downstairs. Call me any time you need me."

The day came when I finally felt well enough to get out of bed, and I wanted most of all to go to the cemetery. But Aunt Monique stopped me. "Dear, when you have your strength back, we'll go together," she said to me gently. I didn't answer, but I was determined to visit my mother's burial place. In the house, everywhere I looked I felt the absence of my mother. I was so close to her; we'd been like two friends. I would help her in any way I could, cooking and housekeeping, and often I would stand beside her watching and learning from her. And she would tell me what a good daughter I was to her.

Very early one morning, before sunrise, quietly so no one would know, I slipped out of the house and walked quickly to the cemetery. I looked down at my mother's grave and felt as if the earth had devoured her. From that day, every morning before sunrise I would visit the cemetery and stay there for a long period of time. And in mourning my mother I sank into a deep depression. The world could give me nothing; it felt alien to me, and I cut myself off from it.

*   *   *

"Excuse me." A plump elderly woman who'd been sitting in the train beside me pushed past. As soon as I'd given any sign of being awake she'd begun to talk and move around in her seat, complaining about everything. "It's such a long way to the Gaspé... I'm already tired... The weather will probably be rainy there... I can't sleep on trains, it's too noisy... I don't know what to do with myself until tomorrow... God, it's so dark outside..." Her constant complaining got on my nerves. I excused myself and went off to the dining car.

To my surprise, Noel was sitting there reading a book. He didn't notice me arrive. I sat down quietly on a seat nearby and ordered tea. Noel heard my voice. "You couldn't sleep either," he said, and took a seat close to mine.

"I can never sleep on a train. I just wanted to rest a little bit, but there's an older woman beside me and she talks non-stop and complains about everything."

"These people who live alone, when they see someone, they want to talk and talk."

"I wouldn't have minded chatting with her. But it was a monologue, and she never stopped talking. Mostly I didn't like her constant whining."

"Now it's my turn to complain," Noel said with a touch of sarcasm.

"Go ahead."

"If you didn't want to sleep, why did you leave the dining car and end our conversation."

"You saw me; I was exhausted. As I said, I just wanted to have a little rest."

"If you want to rest, why don't you go and take my seat, since I'll be here all night. Come with me and I'll show you where it is."

"Maybe later; I just ordered a tea." As I waited for it to arrive I studied Noel closely. I felt as if I'd known him for such a long time and that he was the type of person I could trust utterly. I wanted to know more about him. "Concerning your mother's love story," I asked, "what else can you tell me about Noel, the Indian boy."

"There's not much more to say," Noel replied.

"Okay. Then talk about yourself and your painting."

"You never say anything about *you*. All I know is your name's Lisa and you're from some county in the Gaspé."

"That's not true. I also told you about my parents," I said, and had a sip of my tea. Noel looked at me, his face lit up with admiration. "And I also know you're a beautiful woman who has the most haunting eyes with their colour of the deepest..." Noel paused.

"Deepest what?" I said, smiling. "I don't know," Noel said, and stopped the waiter to ask for a cup of coffee. Until the coffee arrived, Noel and I sat without speaking, just smiling at each other. I said to him, "Do you want to tell me about your childhood and your painting."

"If I tell you about my life, are you going to talk about your life too?" Noel asked.

"Yes! I'll tell you whatever you want to know."

"Just tell me one thing for now," Noel said impatiently. "Are you married?"

"No," I answered with a smile.

"Excellent! I'm not married either."

"Okay, we're in the same boat, then."

"Well. About my mother, she's a wonderful and a hard-working woman. For as long as I can remember she worked at a small store in our county to put food on the table."

"What about your father?"

"There weren't so many jobs for my father. He worked only in the summertime."

"What did he do?"

"Anything that people would ask him to do. Sometimes he would help out on fishing boats. Sometimes he would go into the woods and cut down trees for the winter. Money was tight, but we were a happy family."

"Do you have any brothers and sisters?"

"No, there's just me."

"That's curious, an Irish family having only one child."

"After my mother gave birth to me, she had some kind of problem and couldn't have any more kids."

"Then you're your mother's blue-eyed boy!"

"Yes, in every sense! But I wasn't spoiled. I had to help my mother with work around the house, and when I was eleven, I began to work summers as a delivery boy. In my youth I learned a lot about poverty; I was aware very early of what it means not to have money. My mother was very gentle, but she was tough on me; and because of her perseverance and determination our lives were better than they could have been. Everything I possess is a result of my mother's hard work and her insight."

What Noel confided to me made me feel closer to him. "Did you enjoy your childhood in the Gaspé?" I asked.

"Oh, Lisa! How can I forget the beautiful memories of my childhood in the Gaspé! I can never forget my happy past. The great land and its forests were so big and so magnificent to me. On hot summer days I could hear the grass grow. The scent of the cedars at night was so strong it made me feel faint. Stars were so close that I always thought I could pick them out of the sky. And the reflection of the white light of the summer moon on the sea would lift me out of myself, while the eternal voice of the sea itself was like a beautiful lullaby in the night. The soft morning breeze that blew as the golden sun awoke and the birds that rose out of the sea, flying and dancing over the water, would intoxicate my little soul. The never-ending miles of seashore and the wildflowers as far as the eyes could see have stayed with me always. As a young boy, often I would go to the shore and lie on my back on a rock looking up at the blue sky and listening to the voice of the sea, the finest music to my ears, and watch the singing birds flying over-head. I would walk barefoot for hours and hours. In the solitariness of the shore I had the feeling that all those things belonged to me as much as I belonged to them. Any-where I go, I get homesick for the Gaspé. When I think of those days, I wish I were a little boy again."

Noel's voice had an engaging quality; it was deep and warm. The way he talked about my birthplace affected me profoundly. "Don't forget, I'm Gaspesian too. I spent my childhood there as well." Noel took my hand gently, but warmly. "I know. We have the same experience of our childhood land and it's almost as though we're related to each other."

I let Noel hold on to my hand. "Talk about our home some more. I like to hear the way you talk. I feel I'm looking at a magnificent picture that you're painting." He took a sip of his coffee; then he paused and gazed at me. There was passion in his eyes.

"Tell me about the fall and the cold winters," I said.

"I don't have to tell you how glorious fall always was; the whole land would change completely with the colours of the leaves... But I could never enjoy the fall as much as I might have – I knew that winter was coming soon."

"Then tell me about the long cold winters," I said teasingly.

"Well, truly, Lisa, I didn't like the cold and wind at all. I always thought that we were being punished for enjoying the beautiful days of summer. I suffered a lot going to school when it was stormy. I got tired of winter, and wished it would never come again."

"I didn't like the storms either," I said, "but I loved the quiet sunny days that came after. I liked to walk through the clean white snow and look at the whiteness of the hills and the snow-covered evergreens. I loved everything about the Gaspé."

The chubby old woman who had the seat beside me in the coach entered the dining car. As soon as she saw me she sat down and began to talk. I slid closer to Noel and whispered in his ear, "She's the one who was sitting beside me and grumbling all the time. I'm leaving now, but I'll see you later." I got up and left the car.

I went back to my seat and sank into it. I was hoping to rest, but the past once more began to race in front of my eyes.

*　　*　　*

Early every morning, when the sun hadn't yet risen from the sea, I would set off on my walk to the cemetery. One day I heard someone calling my name. "Bonjour, Lisa. Where are you going this early in the morning?" a woman asked me in a gentle voice. I turned around to find Mme.

Chouinard standing close by.

"Bonjour, Mme. Chouinard. I'm going to the cemetery to visit my mother's grave."

She tenderly put her hand on my shoulder. "Chérie, please come with me to my house; I want to talk to you."

"No, thank you," I replied firmly. "I want to go and see my mother."

"I understand, but please first come to my house. Then after, you and I will go to the cemetery together."

"Please, I want to go by myself."

"That's fine," she said kindly, "but could you just spare me a few minutes at my house."

Reluctantly I went with Mme. Chouinard. She offered me some breakfast. I didn't have any appetite for food, but she insisted; I had a little bit, and was anxious to leave the house. She took my hand and sat down beside me. Looking into my eyes sympathetically she said, "If I talk to you for a few minutes, will you promise you'll listen to me carefully?"

"Please say whatever you wish to say," I answered.

"Chérie, I understand your pain and I know how much you're suffering and how lonesome you are. No one can replace your mother. But listen, dear, you have to face reality and stand up to your responsibilities. I was in the room when your mother died. I overheard you promise to look after your sisters and your papa. But you don't even look after yourself. Your poor Aunt Monique and a few of the neighbour women are the ones looking after all of you. Think, how long can they keep doing this? Your father must go to work somewhere else to put food on the table. Poor man, he lost the woman that was not only his love: she was the mother of his children and the head of his household.

He is suffering a lot and yet is very worried about you. Think of your two little sisters: they lost not only their mother, they lost you too. They can't reach you. I love you, chérie, but I just wanted to tell you that we all have responsibilities towards ourselves and towards others."

Then she took me in her arms. Mme. Chouinard's words shocked me, and I began to sob loudly. When I'd stopped crying I left her house, ran all the way to the cemetery and sat down beside my mother's grave. I stayed there for a long time and asked myself, "Should I spend the rest of my life grieving for my mother, or should I get on with my life?" I thought of the promise I'd made to her, and I came to the conclusion that I had to be brave and continue on my lonesome road without the help of others. I had to do whatever my mother asked me to do. Suddenly I felt myself emerging from the darkness of my inner world; I realized that I belonged at home with my father and two sisters, whom I'd been neglecting. I got up and ran home.

"Nicole, Carole, Papa, where are you?" I shouted, and ran to the kitchen. They were having breakfast. I threw myself into my father's arms and began to cry. "Oh, Papa, I'm so sorry! From now on I'll look after everything. Don't worry about us. Please go back to work!"

He kissed me and said. "I'm not going back to my old job. I have to find something here in our village to be near all of you, so I can help you and do whatever you need me to do." I left my father's arms and rushed to my sisters; I threw my arms around them, my face all wet with tears. "From now on we're going to be a happy family and work together," I said. Carole and Nicole were so excited that I was actually talking to them. They kissed me and agreed to do anything I wanted them to do.

My father's and my two sisters' words made me feel good about myself. I felt an expanded sense of power and authority, and I held my head high.

After breakfast, I began to organize the house the way my mother used to do. I called Nicole and Carole into the living room and said, "Both of you, listen to me carefully. From now on, Carole you're responsible for feeding the chickens, and Nicole you have to gather the eggs. And for the work around the house, when I wash the dishes, Carole you have to dry them, and Nicole you have to clean the table." Nicole interrupted me and said, "The table's too high for me; I can't clean it." I looked at her and with a smile said, "Okay, but when I cook, both of you stand beside me the way I used to stand beside Mamma. You'll watch me and also help me. You have to bring me whatever I might need. I don't want Aunt Monique cooking for us anymore. Poor Aunty, she has to look after her house and her own family too; she's done a lot for us since Mamma's been gone. We have to take care of ourselves." And with that I put the apron on and began to prepare something for our lunch.

"Lisa, what are you doing?" Aunt Monique asked as she entered the kitchen carrying a big fish.

"I'm making our lunch."

"Don't you want me to cook for you anymore?"

"Thank you, Aunty, for everything you've done," I said, "but from now on *I'll* look after us. But I'm grateful for the fish." And Aunt Monique, with a puzzled look, handed it to me.

My father, who was sitting on the porch smoking a cigarette, called Aunt Monique outside. I overheard him telling her, "Say nothing to Lisa; please let her do whatever she wants to do. I think a miracle has happened. She's her old self again."

Aunty said, "Thank God. I just hope she won't fall back into her sadness."

"I hope so too. Don't worry. I'm here, and I'll watch her carefully and keep you informed."

"Do you think you can find a job for yourself here?" Aunt Monique asked.

"Our neighbour Mark told me I can work with him."

"You mean Diane's husband."

"Yes."

"That's very nice of him. Can you work as a carpenter?"

"I can be his assistant. But first I want to be sure that Lisa is doing all right."

I felt bad for putting my father in a situation where he had to worry about me all the time. I ran out to the veranda, kissed him and said, "Don't worry, Papa, I'm just fine!"

He said to my aunt, "Monique, I don't know how I can thank you for all your help."

"Don't say anything," she answered. "We're all related to each other. The loss of my sister is a loss for all of us. God will help us, and we have to help each other."

We all went back inside. I began to clean the fish; Nicole and Carole stood beside me and watched me carefully, and Aunt Monique came over, kissed each of us and said, "I'm so proud of you girls." I looked at Aunt Monique closely and noticed that she'd lost a lot of weight and seemed old and worn. She'd been a beautiful warm woman with the happiest gray eyes and a charming smile. "What happened to her sweet face?" I thought to myself. "The death of my mother has crushed her. Although she doesn't talk about it with us, I'm sure when she goes home she sits alone at the kitchen table and cries for her sister."

I stopped cleaning the fish, put my arms around her and kissed her. "Oh, Aunty, you must have suffered so much since Mamma died." Aunt Monique, who was always so quiet and always said that the death of her sister was God's will, burst into tears. "Marie-Josée wasn't only my older sister, she was like a mother to me. I miss her terribly."

My father, who was headed back to the porch, heard Aunt Monique's sobbing and came into the kitchen to put his arms around her. "Oh, Monique. You're stronger than any of us. You have such deep faith. Please don't cry; we all need you."

We sat down at the table. Aunt Monique wiped away her tears.

"As you know, Lisa, we were six kids; four boys and two girls. The boys were older than your mother and me; I was the baby. Our parents were hard-working people, especially our mother: she was a strong-minded woman and we children had the greatest respect for her. Our father was a fisherman; he would leave the house before sunrise and come back after sunset. Our mother ran the entire household. She would begin working before Papa left the house and she was the last one in bed at night.

"I never saw my mother sit and relax. She worked constantly indoors and outdoors, feeding the chickens, looking after the other animals, feeding them, milking them, taking care of the vegetable garden and potato field – and she had to look after six kids too. She had a hard life, but the smile never left her beautiful face. Isn't that so, Jack?"

My father nodded his head. "It's all true, Monique. Your mother had the most beautiful smile and was a wonderful soul, a hard-working powerful woman. Even in her old age she was tough."

Aunt Monique smiled. "She was tough and she taught us to be strong too. But she had a hard life with my father. I don't want to say bad things about Father, especially since he's dead. But I can't deny how hard life was for my mother. In the winter, when there were no jobs for my father, because the boats couldn't go out, he'd stay home and drink, and most of the time he'd get nasty. My poor mother, she had to put up with him. As we grew older we began to help our parents, but when my eldest brother couldn't find a permanent job in our village and left to live out west, Father grew nastier. Gradually the three other brothers left the house too and settled out west. My father's drinking got even worse. He was aggressive when he drank, and the day came when he started beating my mother."

Aunt Monique unbuttoned her blouse at the neck as if she were being suffocated by the story she was telling us. I ran and brought her a glass of water; she took a sip and continued her story.

"Whenever our father started to shout at our mother, we knew that a beating was coming. Marie-Josée would take my hand and we'd run and hide in the barn, until our mother, with her bruised body, would come and get us. 'You can come on out now,' she'd say. 'He's gone to bed.'

"She'd be hurting for days, but she didn't want any of the neighbours to know about the beating. She didn't want to be an object of pity. And she'd defend our father to us. 'Deep inside he's a good man; it's the alcohol that makes him sick and savage. Go pray for him and ask God to guide him.'

"Every night I would pray for my father; it was then that I began to feel close to God, and my faith grew stronger. In those hard times Marie-Josée was the one who always helped and comforted me. It was Marie-Josée who saved my life, who didn't let me drown in grief and despair. She was like a rock, and I could lean on her. She would always cheer me up when I was sad. And the situation at home went from bad to worse; Father drank all the time, until finally his heart failed him. Our mother grieved and still believed that our father deep down inside was a good man. It took her time to get over her sorrow and put her life back in order. But after a while, Mother, Marie-Josée and I were living peacefully together, working hard and helping each other, until..." Aunt Monique pointed at my father with a pleasant smile. "Until you, Jack, married my sister."

"Please, Aunty," I said, "I want to know more about you and my mother. How did she help you? How strong was she?"

"She was not only a good sister to me, she was a wonderful daughter to our mother too. She didn't forget us when she got married. She helped us in any way she could. After the death of our mother, Marie-Josée became like a mother to me, and when I got married and had my first child she was always there to guide me and help me. She was a smart woman, too. When I had my second daughter and she'd had three she said to me, 'Let's not allow our daughters to work, get married, have babies and grow old in this little village. We have to make sure they're educated and see something of the world, and if they want to come back here and help others, then they're welcome to.' Marie-Josée was not only my sister, she was my brother, my father, my mother, my friend, my mentor. She was everything to me. After her I have no one except you."

Aunt Monique began to sob again, and in a low voice

said, "Soon I'm going to have a third baby myself –"

Carole and Nicole started to shriek. "No! No, Aunt Monique!" Nicole cried. "You're going to die like Mamma! God will take you away from us too!" Aunt Monique threw her arms around both of them. "No, my dears, I'm not going to die. Women are always giving birth to babies and they don't die."

"Then how come Mamma died?" Nicole asked.

"There was a problem with the baby."

"No! You said it was the wish of God. I don't like God. God killed my Mamma!"

"Never ever say those things," Aunt Monique said sharply. "Bite your tongue!"

"No, I *will* say them. And I'll never pray again!"

"We should wash your mouth out with soap. You should kneel down and ask for God's forgiveness."

"I'm not going to do that," Nicole shouted back, and sobbing she ran upstairs and closed the door behind her. Aunt Monique started after her, but my father stopped her. "Leave her be. She's suffering like all of us from the death of Marie-Josée. After all, she's only a child, and she misses her mother."

"Still, she shouldn't say those things. It's sacrilege."

"She doesn't know what she's saying."

"You know, Jack, I think you're not a true believer," Aunt Monique said angrily. She got up to leave and said to us, "I know you're all good girls. You have to talk to Nicole and the three of you must never forget your prayers at night and must all come to church on Sunday. Lisa, dear, you have to have faith. Remember, faith helps heal the wounds in your soul." She kissed us and left the house.

Once she was gone, Nicole came back down to the

kitchen. My father said, "You shouldn't say things like that to your aunt. You know how pious she is."

Quickly I defended Nicole. "It's not her fault. Aunty said women are always giving birth to babies and they don't die, and Nicole couldn't understand why God wanted to take only Mamma away. Actually, I want to know too: why did God take our Mamma away from us?" My father looked away and said nothing.

I began to gut the fish for our lunch, but when I saw blood all over my hands, I got frightened: it reminded me of the day my mother died, the day I went to her bedroom to see her, how everything I saw was covered in blood, how everything was red.

Hurriedly I washed my hands and rushed out of the kitchen. My father, who'd been pacing back and forth, followed me and called out, "Lisa, are you okay, my dear? What's the matter?"

"Oh, Papa, I can't stand blood. It makes me sick! You didn't see what I saw in Mamma's bed. Everything was red and soaked in her blood."

My father put his arms around my shoulders. "My dear, I can imagine the heartbreak you went through. But you can't run away any time you see blood. You have to remember that blood is a sign of life. As long as blood is running in our veins, we're alive. Your mother's death will leave its mark forever, but you have to carry on. Please think about it and try to get over your fear. We all need you; we need each other. Do you want to come back to the kitchen with me and we'll gut the fish together?"

From that day my life took another direction. I was only eleven years old, but I had to act like a young mature woman, looking after my two young sisters and my father.

In a short period of time I grew ten years older. I became a woman with a load of responsibilities and had to do my job perfectly. After all, I had promised my mother. During the day I was busy with housework and taking care of my sisters and my father. But when everyone went to bed, I felt the loneliness of life without my mother. I would lie awake and think over and over about my responsibilities. Often I'd be afraid of the next day. Sometimes in the middle of the night I would panic, get up from my bed, go to the kitchen and prepare breakfast for the morning. Sometimes I would picture my mother on her deathbed telling me, "I know you can do it. You're a brave girl. You can do it." Her voice and her image pushed me to bear the responsibility that she'd placed on my shoulders. Still, holding on to it was no easy task. Once my mother had told me that before me she'd had a girl whom she'd named Karine, but who died when she was only six months old. At night when I was alone and feeling insecure I would talk to my unknown sister. "Karine, I wish you were alive. You'd be older than me, you could have taken responsibility for our home."

I was working around the house and doing whatever my mother used to do, but I didn't want my mother's life. I would remember what she once said to my Aunt Monique: "Let's not allow our daughters to work, get married, have babies and grow old in this little village. We have to make sure they're educated and see something of the world..." The words "We have to make sure they're educated" became the motivation in my life. Also, I didn't want my sisters learning just how to cook and keep house. I wanted them to be educated too.

Summer had passed, and with the glorious fall weather school had begun. I was worried about how the kids there would treat us. Everyone in the village knew that we'd lost our mother, and I was afraid that people had told their children to be nice to us out of pity. The night before school began I sat with Carole and Nicole and explained to them how to react to the kids at school, how to be gentle and polite, yet firm, how not to allow the kids to feel sorry for them.

Between going to school and being with our friends and having our homework to do, life became more meaningful for all of us. Winter was coming and Father did not have much work to do; most of the time he was at home and helping me around the house. He'd learned how to cook, and in the cold days of winter, when we came back home from school Father had already prepared food and the house was warm and pleasant. We were managing our lives without the help of others. Aunt Monique and our neighbours were filled with admiration for us; often they would stop me on the road and tell me how proud they were of me. There wasn't much money, but somehow we managed the affairs of the house.

During the Christmas holidays I tried hard to make everyone happy, but at night I was up and thinking of my mother and all the joyful years we'd had together. I was sure each member of our family had the same feeling, but in order not to make the others sad we all tried hard to look happy.

We were excited when the smells of spring filled the air, especially Father, who would get work again and earn some money. It was on one of those beautiful sunny days of April that we came back from school and found our neighbour Diane with a young woman sitting in the kitchen and my father picking up empty coffee cups from the table.

Suddenly I felt nervous. "What's going on?" I asked. "Is everything okay?"

My father gently answered, "Yes, dear."

I looked at Diane and was on the point of asking her about the young woman when she said, "This is Rita, my cousin. She's visiting from the next county, and she'll be staying with me for a month. I brought her here to see you; I talk a lot about you girls."

The next day when we arrived back from school, I saw Rita leaving our house. She was trying to hide herself from us, but it was too late. I ran inside; I saw my father hurriedly picking up two coffee cups from the kitchen table and putting them in the sink. "What was she doing here?" I asked him without even saying hello. "Well," Father said, "since I'm going to begin working with Mark, Diane asked Rita to come to our home and help out."

"We don't need any help. We've managed so far and we can carry on with our lives without help from any stranger."

"I can't say no to Diane; I'm going to be working with her husband."

"It has nothing to do with your job. I don't want any strangers in our home," I said angrily, and went upstairs. This was the first time in my life that I confronted my father.

The next day, when we came back from school Rita was sitting beside my father in the kitchen drinking coffee. For the first time I looked at Rita carefully. She was young and in certain ways attractive. The first thing you couldn't help notice was her bosom, since she revealingly left the top buttons on her shirt open. She had a round face, and long dark hair scattered over her shoulders. But the trouble was her eyes: they were yellowish and small, and there was something malicious about them. That afternoon she stayed for dinner. At the table I kept looking questioningly at Rita; I didn't know what she was doing in our home. But she ignored me completely and kept busy with Carole. After dinner, as if she were the head of our family, she cleaned the table and asked Carole to bring her homework; she worked with her for a long time. That night she stayed with us until late. I had a feeling that something was going on, but I couldn't figure out exactly what it was.

The whole night I was up thinking of Rita. "Who is she?" I wondered. "Why is she coming to our home and why doesn't my father mind?"

The next day, as we made our way back from school, I asked Carole and Nicole to go on ahead and I stopped in at Aunt Monique's house. She was breastfeeding her new baby girl when I knocked on the door. She looked at me in surprise and said, "Is everything okay?"

"I'm afraid not," I replied. She put the baby in her cradle. She took my hand and asked me to go with her into the kitchen, where we sat on a bench close to each other. "What's wrong, chérie?" she said, putting her hand on my shoulder. I looked into her eyes and asked, "Do you know this Rita? Who is she? Why is she coming to our home?"

Aunt Monique took me in her arms and gently said, "Are you ready to hear the truth?"

I pulled myself away, sat up straight and said, "Yes. Please tell me whatever you know."

"Listen, dear," Aunt Monique said. "Men and women need each other; that's just how it is. Your father can't live alone forever; he needs a woman to be with him to share his life and his bed. Rita is going to be his wife and take care of all of you."

I jumped up from the bench and shouted, "Is she going to replace my mother?" and burst out in sobs.

Aunt Monique got up and took me in her arms again; she began to cry too. "Chérie, no one can take your mother's place, you can be sure of that. But your father must have a wife to look after him and the rest of you."

My hands shaking with anger, I said, "*I'm* doing all those things; we don't *need* anyone. Besides, you know what my mother asked me to do before she passed away."

"Please, sit down and listen to me. Do you think it will be easy for me to come to your house and see another woman replacing my sister, Marie-Josée? Of course not, but there's nothing more we can do about it."

"I've managed it so far; I can keep doing it."

"For how long? You have to look after yourself and also your education. Besides, as I said, your father needs a woman to share his life and his bed."

I jumped up from my seat again. "How can he forget my mother so soon? How *can* he?"

I could hear the tears in Aunt Monique's voice. "He'll never, ever forget your mother."

"Do you know this Rita? Have you seen her?"

"I saw her once."

"Where was that?"

"One day Diane and Rita came to my home and Rita told me about herself. She said her husband had died a year ago and she also mentioned that she can't have children."

"Did Diane say anything about my father?"

"No, chérie, but after a few days your father came to see me and he told me that he wanted to marry Rita. He asked for my blessing, and I told him I'd be happy for him. But after he left, I sat down and cried for my sister."

"But you think my father needs a woman."

"We have to face reality," Aunt Monique said, and went to pick up her crying baby from the cradle.

I left the house and went directly to the cemetery, sat down beside my mother's grave and addressed her as though she were alive. "Mamma, I've kept my promise to you and tried hard to do whatever you asked me to do, but Diane and Rita are traitors. I don't know about my father, but *I'll* love you forever."

After a long cry I went home. Rita was cooking something and Father was talking to Carole and Nicole. I just said hello and went upstairs.

Father followed me to my room. "Are you okay, my dear?" he asked tenderly.

"I'm fine. I just want to be alone." That night I didn't go downstairs for supper.

I was unhappy at home and would talk to no one. In the meantime, Rita gained power over me; she grew close to my sisters, and every evening my father, my sisters and Rita would dine together while I stayed in my room. I couldn't stand Rita, and I was sure she felt the same way towards me.

One afternoon when we'd come back from school, Father told us that he'd be leaving the village for a couple of days. He mentioned that from time to time Diane would come to check on us. I said we could manage for ourselves, and we didn't need Diane.

Late Sunday afternoon, when I was cooking dinner, Father arrived home with Rita and they had several suitcases with them. Before I had time to rush upstairs to my room, Father took my hand and said, "Please, all of you, sit. I have an announcement to make. Rita and

I are married, and now she'll be a mother to you. I hope we'll be a happy family again."

I looked at my father and said nothing. Rita hugged Carole and Nicole, but when she came to kiss me I moved away from her.

Life grew more and more difficult for me; I was a stranger in my own home. Rita captured the attention of my sisters and my father; she had isolated me from doing anything around the house or having any opinion. I was left to my lonely world. I would go to school, come back home, go to my room and be alone. Often Nicole would bring a meal to my room, and I would eat by myself.

Rita was a manipulator and a conniving woman. When my father was at home, Rita was as kind and gentle to me as could be; she would talk softly and lovingly. But when father wasn't around, she would insult me. I hated it when she took a superior tone with me. Whatever I did was wrong. Her voice was so sharp and hostile to me, it was like an incision. She always filled me with terror. Since she didn't speak English I was not allowed to carry on a conversation in English with my father. Anything that might remind me of my mother disappeared; she removed all signs of her from our home. I saw a side of Rita that no one in my family could see. I was sure that she hated me, and I was not able to love her either. I became more and more withdrawn and cut myself off from the rest of my family. I took refuge in my room, and books were my sole companions.

To feel less lonely, I began to write down all the events of the day, and this helped me a lot. I also created an imaginary friend for myself and started to write to her everything that had happened to me in the course of my life. And I read poetry, reciting the lines aloud to soothe my loneliness.

Since I wanted no one to read my writings, I would hide my notes between my pillow and its case. My writings were the most important thing in my life. My diary was like a holy book to me; it was the reflection of my lonely soul.

At school one day I suddenly felt ill, and the teacher suggested I go home and rest. When I arrived home, as usual I ran upstairs to my room. Diane and Rita were there; Diane had my diary in her hands, she was translating aloud for Rita. I rushed in and snatched the notebook from Diane. I was so angry I couldn't control myself; I grabbed Diane's hair and shouted, "You're thieves, both of you!" Rita kicked me so hard I fell on the floor. Pain shot through my ribs. I got up and began to pull at Rita's hair. Somehow I managed to get out of the room and out of the house. With my dear diary in my hands, shivering with fever and sobbing, I managed to make it to Aunt Monique's house.

I told Aunt Monique the whole story. She put me to bed, telling me to rest and to try to be calm, but I could see the rage on her face. I ate some vegetable soup she'd made, and then I fell asleep.

I woke up to the sound of my aunt's loud angry voice; she was shouting at my father. "Jack, you should be ashamed of yourself, coming here to rebuke your daughter. Do you know what really happened?" I heard my father's furious voice. "Yes, that daughter of mine fought with my wife and my neighbour. She pulled their hair."

"And do you know why?"

"Of course I know. Lisa came home early from school and found Rita cleaning her room and went crazy." Aunt Monique yelled back at him, "She's a liar, she's a terrible woman." This was the first time in my life I'd heard my father and my aunt talking to each other with no respect. At last Aunt Monique asked my father to sit down and listen to her. She described the whole event to my father, and then asked, "Jack, have you ever looked carefully at your daughter? Since you got married and Rita came into your home, there's no freshness in her face anymore. She looks sick and depressed. The sparkle is gone from her eyes."

My father answered, "It's not Rita's fault. Lisa has become rebellious. She talks to no one at home."

"And do you know why? Because Rita took everything away from Lisa and pushed her aside. She has no mother, no power, and no right to say a word of her own, and now above all she has no privacy. She feels all alone in the world."

"What do you mean, no privacy? She has her room."

"Sure, she has a tiny room to herself, which is smaller than a bathroom, but she's not secure in that place either. Your wife has invaded her privacy. Her notebook was everything to her; it was her soul, and Rita stole it from her."

"What do you think we should do?"

"Nothing. Go home until your wife comes here and apologizes to Lisa. Rita has to change her attitude towards her."

"I don't know why none of you like poor Rita," my father said.

Aunt Monique replied sharply, "We have our reasons. For one thing, Rita is a scheming woman. Recently I found out that your marriage was already planned before you knew anything about it. Pushing Lisa aside was also part of that plan." My father said nothing more, and quietly left the house.

I stayed at my aunt's house for two weeks and there was

no news of my father and Rita. I would see my sisters at school, but we would not talk about my living arrangements. Finally, one Sunday afternoon when Aunt Monique and I were having tea and cake, my father and Rita came to see me. My aunt asked me to leave the kitchen and go upstairs. After half an hour she called me to down to the kitchen and said, "Lisa, dear, Rita wants to say something to you." Rita looked at me with those vicious little eyes, and since I couldn't look back into hers, I simply lowered my head. Reluctantly she said, "I'm sorry. From now on, I'll never go to your room without your permission."

My father looked over at Rita. "Do you want to say something else?" "Oh yes, from now on we'll be friends."

My father asked me if I wanted to say something also. I looked at my aunt; she nodded her head. "I'm sorry, too, that I lost my temper." And the three of us went home.

My real misery began on that day.

Rita was the same nasty woman, and her attitude towards me was the same. To my disappointment, I noticed that our neighbours, who had always been nice to me, had changed their behaviour too: they would no longer talk to me. Soon I found out that Rita had poisoned their minds against me. She'd told them that I had strange manners and was not normal.

One day Rita announced that her younger brother was coming from Calgary for a visit and would be spending two weeks in our home. She got busy preparing a room for him and baking, and had no time to harass me.

A week later, Rita's brother arrived. It was early evening and I was in my room doing homework when Rita called up to me. "Lisa, come down, I want you to meet my brother."

Unwillingly I went downstairs. I didn't want to look at Rita – as always my eyes were fixed on the floor, but I managed to glance at her brother. He was a young, short, heavy man; his face resembled Rita's, especially his eyes, vicious and cruel. I said hello and went back to my room.

At dinner, Rita tried to be charming and nice to me. Her brother, who was called Chris, talked and joked constantly. I didn't like his artificially happy expression. After what was to me a boring dinner, I got up to go to my room. My father stopped me and whispered in my ear. "With Chris here, dear, please come down every night and have dinner with us."

"I'll do my best, papa," I said.

The next day, as I was going to my room, Chris asked me to stay and talk to him. Politely I excused myself. After an hour I heard someone knocking at my door; before I could say anything, Chris came into the room and sat on the edge of my bed. He began to chat in too friendly a way; I didn't care for his attitude and also I didn't want him getting personal. I asked him to leave the room, but he ignored me. I said, "Don't you see I'm busy with my homework?"

Three more times over the next few days he came to my room, and each time I asked him to leave. Once he touched my hair. "You have such nice hair," he said. I pulled away. I didn't want him around me. I didn't like him, and I would stay away from him as much as I could – until that horrifying Sunday.

The weather was pleasant, and my father, Rita and my sisters went off to visit friends. They asked me to go with them, but as much as I wanted to be with my father and sisters, I didn't want to spend my Sunday with Rita and her brother. I was alone at home; I enjoyed having the house to myself. Suddenly in the early afternoon the weather changed. It began to pour rain, and I went to my room to lie down. After a few minutes I heard footsteps on the stairway. I got up to see who was coming up the stairs when the door of my room opened and Chris walked in. I could feel those cruel little eyes on me. He came towards me and pushed me backwards. I tried to fend him off with my fists and began to scream. He grew enraged and threw himself at me. Then he pushed me down on the bed and forced himself on me.

As he left the room he pointed a finger at me. "You'd better keep your mouth shut. Because everyone knows you hate my sister. So no one's gonna believe you." The whole event happened so fast, I didn't have time to understand.

I had no emotions; I was beyond feeling. I was frozen; my body was death. I felt as if I'd observed a horrendous incident some place outside myself. The anguish of being overpowered suffocated me. I'll never forget how I cried out, but no one was there to hear me.

My privacy had been violated, but the whole afternoon it was me who felt guilty, sad, angry and dirty. I felt I'd disgraced my family; I was ashamed of myself. The sound of silence seemed almost threatening to me. I buried my face in the pillow, and through my loud sobs I heard my mother's tender voice again. "You're a strong girl; I'm proud of you." All of a sudden I felt my power return. I got up from the bed, washed my body, sat back down on the bed and began to think. I realized that Rita, her brother, the neighbours, the village, everything around me was against me. I decided to fight my way out of it. I thought, "I have to be strong like the sea; I should not feel sorry for myself.

I have to leave my father's house, but before I go there's something I have to do." I said to myself, "I will not live in this house anymore, but before I go I have to have my revenge."

I gathered all the belongings I needed and stuffed them in a cotton sack, which I hid under a bush outside the house. I had a strange feeling: on the one hand I was acting like a strong girl determined to fight back and not feel sorry for herself; on the other, I felt sorry for a young girl who was a victim of injustice. Finally I fixed my hair nicely, put on my Sunday dress and waited for the others. I knew exactly what I was planning to do, and I had no sense of fear.

In the evening, my family all returned home. Since they'd had their dinner at the friends' house, Nicole and Carole went to bed. I went to their room and kissed them; I told them how much I loved them. I heard my father's voice. I needed badly to go downstairs, throw myself into his arms and tell him what had happened to me. I needed him to comfort me and make me feel secure and punish Chris, but I also needed my own revenge. No one could punish Chris better than me, no one's heart was like mine and no one could understand my pain better than me.

I came downstairs and calmly entered the kitchen, greeting all of them in a friendly manner. My father seemed happy to see me; I smiled at him, and took deep breaths to control my desire to cry. I said, "Papa, would you like me to make tea?"

"Please, my dear," he said happily, and for the first time since my mother's death got out his fiddle and began to play. Rita put the kettle on the stove. I looked at her and said, "No, you go sit down and I'll make the tea." My father asked her to let me serve them, and she sat down beside him. Chris sat opposite my father and Rita; he was cheerful and talkative, as if he'd done nothing to me.

When the water boiled I made the tea. I poured a cup for my father and one for Rita. I moved close to Chris, gazed into his vicious eyes and asked with a friendly smile, "Do you want tea too?" He looked at me victoriously. "Yes, please."

I picked up a big mug, filled it with boiling water and on top sprinkled a little tea. My hands were shaking, but I managed to control myself, thinking, "Don't be afraid: remember when he came to your room and how savagely he molested you. *He* wasn't shaking." I walked over to Chris with the steaming mug in my hand. My father was busy playing the fiddle and Rita was clapping her hands. I got closer to Chris and suddenly, as if I'd slipped on something, I dumped all the blistering hot water over his groin.

"Oh God, I'm sorry!" I called out. "It was an accident! It was an accident!" Chris had jumped up and was tearing off his pants, screaming. And I was thinking, "The only response to violence is violence. It's the only way, the only way..."

That moment I felt I grew another ten years older. I rushed out, picked up my sack, and left my father's home for good.

*   *   *

"You told me you can't sleep on trains." I opened my eyes; Noel was standing near me. I was amazed I hadn't noticed him. I pulled myself together. "Whatever I said to you, it's true. I can't sleep on a train. I was just resting, and my thoughts were far away. But you took me by surprise."

"Sorry." he said with smile. "I just wanted to give you some good news."

"It had better be good news."

"Oh, yes! The chatty woman found someone in the dining car and she's yakking away to him now. I think she'll stay there for the rest of the night. We don't need to go back there; we can stay here and talk."

Noel sat beside me and put his hand on my shoulder. After a pause he looked deep into my eyes and said, "Lisa, can I tell you a secret?"

"Sure, go ahead."

"You won't believe it."

"Try me."

"How can I put it? I've been rehearsing the sentence I want to say to you, but I can't say it."

"Whatever you want to say, just say it!" I said eagerly. Noel took both my hands and with a childlike look on his face said, "Listen, Lisa. When you left the dining car to go and rest, I suddenly felt so lonesome. I missed you terribly." He pressed my hand.

I burst out laughing. "You missed me for just this short period of time – it's hard to believe."

Noel looked at me sadly. "I knew you wouldn't believe me."

"Noel," I said tenderly. "I believe you, but you have to learn to be good company to yourself. Life is a road on which you're always alone, even when you're with a hundred people."

"I don't need you to give me philosophical advice," he said curtly. "I just wanted to tell you I missed you a lot." His voice softened. "And I have to tell you something else, whether you like it or not." He took me in his arms.

"Lisa, the moment you raised your head from the table in the dining car and looked at me with those beautiful soft eyes, I felt something warm inside me. If you want, you can call it love – yes, I'm in love with you."

He pressed his lips to my neck, put his hands around my waist and kissed me passionately. The blood rushed to my face. I looked deep into his blue eyes. "Are you sure of what you're saying."

"Oh yes! Yes, Lisa. I'm positive."

"But you don't know me."

"You know *me,* and that's enough for me."

"How many times have you fallen in love this way?"

He hesitated. "Just once. This is the second."

"What happened to your first love?"

"Do you really want to know?"

"Of course I want to know."

"It's a long story."

"It's a long night too," I said with smile. But I couldn't wait to hear his love story. Also I wanted him to talk; I loved listening to him. Noel sighed and gazed at me, passion in his eyes.

"I have to give you some background. As I told you before, I always wanted to be a painter. As a young boy I would draw the shoreline, the forest and the sea, and show them to my mother. She encouraged me and believed in me. She would say that one day I'd be a famous painter like my great-grandfather."

"And are you?" I asked with a smile.

"Not yet, but who knows, maybe some day. I'm working hard to achieve my goal."

He resumed his story. "One day in late spring, when I came home from school my mother said, 'Listen, dear, I have big news for you.'

"I got so nervous I couldn't ask about the news. When she saw my frightened face, she smiled. 'Don't be scared, it's not bad news. Actually it's good news about your future.'

"My father, who was sitting next to my mother, got annoyed. 'Just tell him, would you! What is this nonsense?'

"'Okay, okay, I'll tell him. I'm so excited!' She took my hand. 'Dear, we're going to Montreal to live. One of my cousins found good jobs for me and your father.'

"'What kind of jobs? When are we going?'

"'Your father and I are going to be working in a nursing home. But first we have to see the people in Montreal.'

"'And what am *I* going to do?'

"'You'll stay with Uncle Tony for a week,' she said, and the next day they took off to Montreal.

"During the week with my Uncle Tony I felt confused and bewildered. I didn't want my parents to take me away from my beloved Gaspé. My uncle, seeing me so unhappy, promised to take me on a fishing trip out to sea.

"That Saturday before sunrise, my uncle and I and one of his partners boarded the fishing boat and set sail. I'll never forget that remarkable day. It's haunted me all my life. It was the first time it occurred to me that I would be homesick for the sea. The rest of the week I was unhappy and anxious. I didn't want to leave the Gaspé and give up my childhood memories.

"When my parents came back, they'd secured the jobs and had arranged to rent a small apartment. As soon as school let out, we made the move to Montreal. I wanted to stay in my beloved Gaspé for the summer, when the hot sun baked the earth, but I had no choice.

"Montreal was like another world. Coming from a quiet

village to a crowded city was a nightmare for me. It took me a long time to adapt to the new environment, and always I longed for home." Noel paused.

I looked out the window and could see the reflection of dawn on the trees. "It's almost morning. Let's go have coffee," I suggested.

The dining car was quiet; only a few people were there drinking coffee, including the chubby woman. We sat in a corner and ordered breakfast.

When the coffee came, Noel picked up his cup and looked at me intently. I saw love in his eyes.

"Life was hectic in Montreal," he continued. "My parents were doing day and night shifts at the nursing home. One night my mother wouldn't be at home, and one night my father. Although there wasn't that much work at night, and even though their job was mostly washing and cleaning, one of them had to sleep there in case of emergency. Sunday was the only day we were together as a family."

Noel drank more coffee. "Do you want to hear about my own life in Montreal too?"

I pressed his hand. "Of course. I want to hear everything about your life. Please don't feel shy about telling me anything. I want to know you better."

Noel glanced up. "Lisa, look! The sun is up. Look at the blue sky on the horizon. In a couple of hours we'll be in the Gaspé. I can't wait to see the place where I spent the happiest time of my life!"

I looked out. The reflection of the sun on the multi-coloured trees was stunning. We moved close to the window, and holding hands, took in the magnificent view. I turned his face to mine and kissed him passionately. Noel held me in his arms and kissed me back.

When we managed to regain our seats, Noel continued his story.

"I can summarize my life in Montreal in three words," he said: "work, work, work. From the time I got out of bed until late in the evening to go back to bed I was busy working. I was either doing my homework or working for others. Life wasn't easy; to make money you have to work hard. You name it, I was doing it. My parents bought me a second-hand bicycle and on the weekend I would deliver newspapers. Since my mother had a good relationship with the residents of the nursing home, I would go and buy them whatever they needed. In the winter I'd help neighbours shovel the snow off their driveways, in summer I'd mow their lawns and in the fall I'd rake the leaves. What else? Oh yes, I would also help my parents at home."

Noel took a deep breath. I looked at him and playfully said, "Well at least in the spring you didn't have anything to do."

He smiled a bitter smile. "You're wrong there, Lisa: spring was the worst time. It was the end of the school year with all the exams, plus everyone wanted me to clean their yards and rake their dead grass. Do you know how many houses in the neighbourhood I had to clean? I'd rather not even talk about it."

I looked into his deep blue eyes and said, "Okay, don't talk about the work anymore – just tell me what you did with all that money."

Noel smiled. "Well, it's complicated. We were spending half my parents' salary on living expenses and half would go into the bank. Whatever I was making would go directly into our savings as well. My mother would only give me a little spending money each month."

"Did you know why they had to save so much money?" I asked.

"Of course. My mother kept saying we needed to save a lot in order to buy a house in Montreal."

"It wasn't fair to you."

"I used to have the same feeling, and I was often angry with my mother. When I asked her about it, she'd say that prices in Montreal were very high and we really had to save up."

"Do you resent your mother for being that unfair?" I asked. Noel didn't answer; he wanted me to listen to the rest of his story, and I promised not to ask any more questions.

"When I finished high school and began college, my mother didn't want me to work anymore. She wanted me to concentrate on my studies and my painting, but she found a job for me anyway. A rich woman at the nursing home had a granddaughter who wanted to improve her French and her family was looking for a private tutor. My mother recommended me, and I became a French tutor in a rich English home. She was a nice girl, who worked hard – except after a few weeks I couldn't help but notice she'd developed a crush on me. I didn't want to hurt her feelings, so I continued my tutoring for one more week, but after that I told her my schoolwork prevented me from teaching anymore. And that was the end of my tutoring career!"

I smiled. "I don't blame the girl; I'd have been in love with those shy deep eyes too." Noel took my hand and kissed it.

"You can't stop there," I said. "I want to know what else happened."

"You haven't told me anything about *your* life," Noel

answered. "I know nothing about you."

"I promise you I'll tell you everything. But I love listening to you, to your voice. Please don't stop."

"Okay, but I'm not telling you the whole story of my life unless you tell me something about yours too." I agreed. Noel began to talk again, and I was as silent as a shadow.

"After I graduated from college, one Sunday afternoon my mother called me and my father into the living room; she said she had something very important to announce." Suddenly Noel was crying, though not sadly. It took a few moments for him to get his emotions under control.

"We all sat down in the living room, and my mother asked us not to interrupt. Then she turned to me. 'Noel, my dear, I'm sure when you were in high school you were angry at me or maybe sometimes you even hated me for all the hard work I asked you to do. You have to remember that your father and I also worked hard, and we're still working at the same job. What I wanted to tell you is that all the money I've collected all these years is in the bank, and it all belongs to you. There was never any plan to buy a house.'

"My father jumped out of his chair and shouted at my mother, 'Do you know what you're saying?' And my mother replied, 'Yes, I know very well what I'm saying. There will be no home; we have our small house in the Gaspé, and when we retire we'll go back there. Sit down and listen, I'm not finished yet.'

"My father, fuming, sat back in his place and waited for the rest of my mother's announcement. She looked at me with those loving gray eyes and said, 'Noel, dear, I want you to follow your childhood dream. I want you to have this money to go to Paris and continue your painting. I've organized everything for you. An influential relative of someone at the nursing home has arranged for you to be admitted to the Institut there. You'll have a room to yourself, and I'll send you money every month. But if you want to go to university here, that's also fine with me.' Noel looked at me with fresh tears in his eyes. I warmly squeezed his hand. After a moment, he continued.

"The whole thing astonished me. I couldn't imagine in my wildest dreams that my mother, all those years, was putting money aside to send me to Paris to become a painter. Suddenly I was a little boy again, walking on the shore with the birds flying over the water, and my dreams soaring with them above the blue sea.

"I got up from my chair, knelt in front of my mother and began to kiss her worn, hard-working hands. She put them on my hair, as she used to do when I was a little boy, and gently pushed it back. 'Go, my boy, and follow your dreams,' she said. 'My life didn't turn out the way I dreamed it would, but I hope *your* life does.'"

Noel got up from his seat.

"Where are you going?"

"To get a cup of tea. Would you like one too?"

"No. No, thank you."

Noel came back with his tea and squeezed closer to me. "Were you crying when I was gone?"

"No."

"Don't pretend, and don't hide things from me. Tell me why you were crying?"

"When you left, I thought how lucky you are to have such an amazing and devoted mother. I have no mother; I so wish my mother were alive."

The tears ran down my face. Noel took me in his arms. "I'm so sorry; I didn't know that your mother had passed away. You say nothing about yourself. Please talk to me," he said caringly.

I looked at him. I'd known him a matter of hours, but his presence inspired immediate trust in me, and when he asked me to talk about my life, I couldn't say no.

"Noel, let me tell you, things happened to me in my youth that chill me even to think about them today. My mother died when I was only eleven. And part of me died too. All the years that have passed haven't dimmed the memory of the day I saw her soaked in her own blood. She's been dead for so many years, but she's more real to me than ever. She's never gone from my life."

Noel gazed at me and said, "I'm so sorry you lost your mother when you were so young. Would it be too painful to tell me how she died?"

I told Noel all the details of the events on that day as if I were reading a tragic chapter of a book. Often I would become so emotional that Noel would stop me and hold me in his arms. But I wanted him to know everything.

"The death of my mother was only the end of the first chapter of my life. The second one is my responsibilities towards my father and two sisters." I told Noel how well I looked after my family, and he couldn't believe what an enormous job I'd done when I was only eleven years old.

"I'm so proud of you, Lisa. What was the third chapter of your life?"

"You might not want to hear the next chapter; this is where the real misery in my life began."

"If I'm to know you better and understand your pain," he said gently, "then I need to know everything that happened."

"Oh, Noel," I said, my voice trembling. "I don't know

why, but I've been holding onto these awful memories for so long! I can't free myself from them. I can still feel the pain and I can never overcome the horror of how lonely I was then. I can still seem to hear my own long, desperate cry, like thunder piercing the sky at night."

I told him about Rita and her cruelty towards me. But when it came to Chris and what he'd done to me, I couldn't talk. After all those years, the atrocious event was so fresh in my memory that I began to shiver. Noel took me in his arms. "That's okay, dear. If you can't talk about it, then don't."

But I fixed my eyes on the table so as not to look at Noel, as if I had done something wrong, and I told him about Chris and the repulsive thing that *he'd* done. Noel got up from his seat and looked down at me with troubled eyes. "You know that was a crime, don't you?"

"I know now. I didn't know then."

"What did you do?"

"I punished him myself."

"You were so young. What could you do to punish him?"

"I was naïve and I did what I could. But all these years I've been battling with myself. There are moments I feel I should have told my father, even though at that time no one would have believed me. But sometimes I feel that the punishment he got from me was the best."

I took Noel's hand. "Noel, let's go back to our seats and just look at the scenery."

"You don't want to talk about your life anymore?"

"I just want to relax for a while."

"Okay, let's go," Noel said, and we left the dining car holding hands.

I sank down in my seat and Noel sat beside me. "Please put your head on my shoulder; I want to feel you closer to me." He said it so lovingly that I couldn't refuse. The landscape was breathtaking. The colourful trees, the river flowing alongside the train, the sun and the migrating birds all took me away from my painful past. I closed my eyes, and out of the blue I fell asleep.

"Lisa, dear, there's a problem." Noel said.

I opened my eyes. "What happened?" I asked worriedly.

"Nothing's happened. It's just that while you were sleeping the conductor announced that there's a problem with the tracks and the train will be stopping in the next station until it's fixed."

"Do you know how long we have to wait?"

"Some people are saying from eight to ten hours."

"I can't believe it," I said. "Let's go find out." As we got up, the train rang its bell and pulled into a small station. People got up from their seats and off the train, trying to find out about the delay. Finally the conductor emerged from a talk with the stationmaster and announced that we had a wait of at least ten hours. We didn't know what to do. I looked at Noel. "I'm not going to sit in this train for ten hours."

"I'm not going to sit and wait either," Noel said. "Let's get our bags and find somewhere to stay for a day or two."

We went back for our luggage and then stood on the platform, wondering what to do next. I looked around and saw a middle-aged woman with a suitcase standing nearby and looking bewildered. I approached her and asked, "Did you just get off the train too?" She smiled. "No, dear, I was planning to *take* the train, but it seems I have to go back home now."

"Do you live in this village?" I asked.

"I've lived here all my life. I just wanted to go to the Gaspé for a couple of days and visit my cousin."

"Do you know of any place where we can stay the night," I asked. "I can't sit in the train and wait for God knows how many hours. I'm already exhausted."

She looked at me and then over at Noel. "You're not alone, are you?"

"No, I'm with my friend."

"Okay. Both of you can come to my house and stay with me. I have a big room for you. My name's Francine, by the way."

The room was beautiful. We left our suitcases there and went out to find a place to eat. Events were happening so fast that I didn't have time to really understand what was going on. I thought, "I've known Noel not more than ten hours, and I'm going to be sharing a room with him." I was struggling with myself when we stumbled on a small diner. "I think this is the only restaurant in this village," Noel said. "Let's go in."

The few people inside noticed that we were strangers, and greeted us with a friendly Bonjour. I felt comfortable being there. After we ate, when we got up to leave a large group of passengers from the train crowded in. "Lucky we had an early lunch," Noel said. And looking at me with the nicest smile said, "And lucky for me I found you."

I said, "How could you find me, I wasn't lost."

"You were lost in my life, and I'd been looking for you for so long." He took my hand. "Let's go for a walk in the woods."

It was one of those pleasantly warm and quiet autumn days, delicious for walking. The sounds of our footsteps on the dry leaves were the best harmonies to my ears. Noel held my hand tight, as if he were afraid to lose me. I could see a simple joy on his face. After a while we sat down on a mound of dry leaves for a rest. Noel took me in his arms. "Lisa, believe it or not, and as I told you on the train, I'm in love with you."

"You told me you loved a woman before me and that I'm only the second. So I'd like to know all about the first one."

Suddenly his happy features turned gloomy, and he uttered a sigh from deep inside. He rested his head on my shoulder and gazed off into the distance. Then he said, "No matter how much you read about Paris or how many pictures and films you see, when you arrive in the city you're overwhelmed by the beauty of the place. You're confused, not knowing when it's day and when it's night. Life runs through the veins of the city.

"In Paris I had a small room in a building that housed students at the Institut. I had the essential things, and there was a big kitchen at the end of the corridor for all the students to use, and a large dining table.

"The morning I arrived, I went to the kitchen to have some breakfast. It was too early for the rest of the students; everybody was asleep. As I was sitting having my coffee I heard a soft voice. 'Bonjour.' I turned my head to see a beautiful girl coming towards me. 'Bonjour,' I said. She came closer and with a friendly smile said, "You must be a new student." She extended her hand. 'My name's Isabel.' I got up and we shook hands. 'I'm Noel.' I said. 'Enchanté,' we said together.

"She made herself a coffee and sat across from me at the table. She was so beautiful. She had the most trusting face in the world; her azure eyes were large, deep and warm and seemed full of life, almost mesmerizing. She had small, delicate features and she was in her mid-twenties. She had a grace and a manner that set her apart from the crowd. When she talked, you could feel the candour of her soul. And the combination of all those things made me fall in love with her right away."

"Do you always fall in love so easily?" I asked.

"I told you before that I've fallen in love only twice. Isabel was the first love in my life, and now you're the second."

"Then finish telling me about Isabel."

Noel took my hand. "It's a heartbreaking story."

"That's okay. I want to hear it."

"After we had our coffee, Isabel asked me to go out for breakfast at one of the sidewalk cafés. During our conversation she told me she was from a small town in northern Spain. She talked openly about her life and she seemed happy to be eating with me.

"She told me that since it was Sunday and she was free, she would spend the day showing me around Paris. She took me to the Louvre and other museums. She said that I had to visit museums at least twice a week and study the paintings there. She listed histories of art and biographies of great artists that I had to read. By the end of the day I was overwhelmed by all the places we'd seen and all the information she'd provided me with. And we'd become good friends.

"The next day she introduced me to everyone at the Institut. She talked about me as if she'd known me for a long time. That night, on our way back home to our rooms, Isabel asked me to have dinner with her. She cooked, and we ate in her room. She said she didn't like eating in the kitchen with everyone else there. She wanted to be alone with me.

"Her room was similar to mine, but she had given it a feminine touch. There was a small table and two chairs. She had set the table beautifully. After dinner she showed me her paintings. They took my breath away; I was amazed by her talent. Most of her work was in oil, though she'd done some watercolours too. But the most interesting thing to me was the subject matter: almost all of the paintings were of sunflowers. One painting might have a single large sunflower, another, an entire field of them. The last work she showed me was of a large house that was burned almost to the ground and a road to the house filled with sunflowers. I didn't understand it, and I asked Isabel what it meant. And for the first time I saw another side to her personality. Suddenly she grew agitated; her beautiful eyes filled with tears.

"She picked up a chair, turned it around and sat down, lowering her chin to the chair back. 'My father was an opponent of the government in Spain and he was in and out of prison. To him the sunflower was a symbol of freedom. He had planted sunflower seeds in front of our house and lined a road with them; he called it the road to freedom. Gradually, more and more people who were opposed to the dictatorial regime grew sunflowers in front of their houses. Our town became filled with sunflowers. Since the regime couldn't tolerate my father and other people with the same beliefs, one night the secret police set our house on fire. I was visiting my aunt, and when I arrived back home the house was a charred wreck and there was no sign of my parents. They'd both been incinerated in the blaze. The government inspector announced that the fire was an accident, but the townspeople refused to believe it; they spread my parents' ashes along the "road to freedom." Today people from other parts of Spain come to the burned house and the sunflower field. Everyone who visits plants a seed there.'

"Her dear face was wet with tears. 'Since I've lived all these years as if I were dead,' she said sadly, 'my death will be no different from my life.'

"I got up from my chair, raised her up and held her in my arms. I told her how much I loved her and how precious she was to me. But she just asked me to leave.

"The next morning I was hoping to see her in the kitchen, but there was no trace of her. I couldn't find her at the Institut either. I missed her terribly, and I was also worried about her. In the evening when I went home I found her in the kitchen, cooking. She didn't want to talk about the night before, but I could see by her face that she'd cried a lot.

"The following day she was up early, making coffee in the kitchen and talking to one of the students. When she saw me she kissed me and said that we were all going out of town to do scenes from nature. All that day she was cheerful and concentrated on her painting. It didn't take me long to notice that her mood could change from day to day; one day she'd be on top of the world, and the next day so down that no one could as much as talk to her. I loved her dearly, and on the days that she felt down I was miserable too. Often at night after our dinner I would go to my room and work on some project. And sometimes in the middle of the night Isabel would knock at the door, wanting to sleep in my bed because she was afraid to be alone.

"But in spite of Isabel's moods, I thought we were generally a happy couple, very much in love. All the students and teachers were aware of how much we cared about each other, and I was a happy man. I was content with my personal life and I was pleased with my work.

"Isabel's occasional depression was the only thing that worried me. There were days, without any apparent reason, when she would talk to no one and wouldn't come out of her room. And the next day she'd be full of life. I learned to stay away from her and leave her alone when that was what she wanted. When she was better I would tell her lovingly that she had a right to be happy, that she couldn't change the past but that the future could be a different story. I would tell her that she had to accept happiness in any form it might take. And I asked her if she would consider getting professional help – I'd go with her, I said. She would listen carefully and promise me she would, but she never did.

"It was one of those beautiful warm spring days. I had to go out of town with some of my fellow students from the Institut to sketch views of a field. Isabel was aware of it and wanted to join us, yet in the morning when I asked her to get ready she said she had something important to do in town and that I should just go ahead with the others. Her mood seemed all right to me."

Noel suddenly got up. He buried his face in his hands and cried out, "And then she vanished from my life forever!"

I removed his hands from his face, looked into those deep sad eyes and said, "It's okay, Noel. I understand your pain. Come and sit with me and talk, it will release you from your sorrows." I kissed him tenderly. He sat down beside me and took my hand.

"In the afternoon when I came back to the city, I was

so anxious to see Isabel I ran upstairs to tell her how much I'd missed her. There was a policeman standing outside her room. He stopped me, asked me who I was, then suggested I accompany him to the police station. Bewildered, I asked him why. All he said was, 'Please just come to the station; my superior will explain everything.'

"It was there that I found out Isabel had killed herself. She had turned on the gas, and by the time anyone got to her, it was too late. The police sergeant handed me a letter that Isabel had written to me; he also asked me to identify her body. This was the hardest thing I'd ever done in my life. The whole event was like a nightmare, and I wanted to force myself awake from it.

"The sergeant took my arm and led me downstairs to the morgue. Isabel looked so peaceful and beautiful, as she always did when she was asleep. I couldn't believe she was dead. I tried to get closer, to wake her up, but the sergeant stopped me.

"I lost control of myself and pushed past him. I wanted to kiss Isabel, and at the same time I wanted to strangle her. I began to scream, 'I love you and I hate you! You've killed yourself and you've killed me! You killed the girl I love!'

"I have no idea how I got home or how I managed to read her letter. She wanted to be cremated, and have her ashes scattered over the sunflower field near where her parents had burned to death. She also wanted me to notify her relatives. In her letter she mentioned how much she loved me and that since she couldn't free herself from her mental condition, she had to release herself from the agony of it. At the end of the letter she wrote, 'I also wanted to set you free from me and from my misery. It was my pain, not yours.'"

Noel could barely get the words out. I had him lie down and put his head on my lap, and like a lost little boy he began to weep. I couldn't help myself and began to sob too. I looked down into his deep sad eyes and realized how much I cared for him. I stroked his hair. "Talk, Noel. Free yourself from whatever's eating at your soul."

"I had no more emotions," he managed to say. And he went on, "I was beyond feeling. There were no more tears in me. On the one hand I missed Isabel, and on the other, I hated her. Often I would blame myself because I didn't keep her from taking such a terrible step; if only I'd known how severe her condition was. Sometimes I had the feeling that I'd loved a woman who was a murderer. She'd killed a girl who was everything to me. She'd killed herself and ruined my life at the same time. She must have hated herself and her life to be able to commit such a terrible crime.

"Paris without Isabel wasn't Paris for me anymore. Everywhere I went I'd see signs of her. There was no choice for me but to leave. And since I've been back here, I've devoted my life to my art and I'm doing well with my painting and achieving some success...

"Well, now you've heard the whole story of my life, and the important part is that I'm in love with you now, Lisa."

For a while we just there, holding each other's hand. The sun looked like a faded rose and the afternoon was getting a little bit chilly. We were both hungry. We went to the restaurant where we'd had lunch, but it was closed. I said to Noel, "Let's go back to the house and ask Francine if she can give us something to eat. We'll pay her."

To our surprise, Francine had set a nice table for us and prepared a lovely meal. "I knew there'd be nowhere to eat; at night everyone eats at home. The restaurant is open at lunch mostly for train passengers to grab something fast, since not everyone likes to pay all that money to eat in the dining car."

I asked Francine if she would join us. During dinner she proposed that we stay in her home as long as we wanted. "I won't charge a lot. I'll include breakfast and dinner with the room, and you can pay me whatever you like." Then she looked at Noel and said with a wink, "I think you're in love with this woman." Noel nodded his head. "Yes!" he said. "Very much." But during dinner Noel was very quiet, and seemed dejected. When we went up to our room, Noel took a blanket and fell asleep on the sofa.

In the morning at the breakfast table Noel looked fresh and happy, and that cheered me up. He asked Francine questions about the area, the river, and how far we could walk. Francine gave him all the details that we needed for our walk, and as we were leaving the house she handed us two sandwiches for our lunch. We couldn't believe her kindness; we kissed her and set off. "Have fun!" Francine said.

It was another sunny and beautiful day. We began to walk alongside the river. It was lovely and quiet, and we saw few people. After a couple of hours we had our lunch on the shore of the river, and then took a path into the woods.

We walked and walked until no one else was in sight. Noel took me in his arms and began to kiss me; he wanted to make love to me. Although deep inside I wanted him too, I stopped him. Noel looked at me and said, "Love is the most natural thing in the world. There's no reason for you to be afraid." I said nothing. Noel gently lifted me up and lowered me to the fallen leaves. Then his body took shelter in mine until the beating of our hearts was the loudest sound in the forest. We were two people deeply in love.

We stayed in Francine's house for a week, one of the most memorable times of my life. My relationship with Noel grew solid; we were madly in love and enjoying every minute of our lives. Francine was unbelievably nice to us; she became like one of our relatives. Every morning I would go with Noel for a walk, and when we found ourselves alone in the forest, like children we would sing, dance and run after each other. There was life inside us; there was no need to borrow it from elsewhere. I would look at myself in the mirror and see the face of a woman who was well loved. I could also see an inner glow of happiness shining through Noel's eyes. Noel drew a sketch of my face, and also made a beautiful painting of Francine's house. She was thrilled when she saw it. We wanted to be on our way, but Francine insisted that we stay a little longer. She said, "I won't charge you for the additional days. I just want to have you here."

The day after was rainy, and we couldn't go for our walk. After breakfast, we went back to our room. Noel looked at me with a smile and said, "Today's the day we sit at home and read a book. How about reading me the book of your life?" He added, "You never told me what happened to you after you left your father's home. I know nothing about your life after that."

I shrugged my shoulders. "It doesn't make any difference to our relationship." Noel replied, "That may be true, but don't you want me to know more about your past?" It occurred to me that Noel thought I might be trying to hide something from him. "Okay," I said. "Have a seat and listen to me.

"I can never forget the night that I took my revenge on Chris. He was screaming from the burning pain and standing half-naked in front of all of us when I left my father's home. I was running as fast as I could towards Aunt Monique's house when behind me I heard the voice of Élise, one of our relatives, shouting, 'Where are you running?'

"'To Aunt Monique's,' I gasped.

"'I'm on my way there myself.' She grabbed my hand. 'We'll walk together.'

"Aunt Monique was surprised to see us; she asked worriedly, 'Is everything all right?' I began to sob. I told Aunty and Élise that I'd accidentally spilled hot water on Chris's sensitive parts and I would never ever go back home. Aunt Monique looked at my sack suspiciously. 'What's in that bag?' she asked. 'It's my clothes. I packed it earlier in the evening, before the accident happened.' Aunt Monique glanced over at Élise, and both of them left the room. Until they came back I sat there shivering.

"Aunt Monique looked at me and said firmly, 'You'll go and stay with Cousin Élise. No one – I mean no one – must know about where you're living. And you don't leave the house either.'

"'Okay, Aunty. I promise I'll do whatever you say.'

"Cousin Élise said, 'First you have to write a letter to your father and tell him that you're in good hands and that he needn't worry about you.'

"I was so nervous I couldn't concentrate. But Élise helped me write a nice letter to my father and explain to him that I could no longer live in that environment. At the end of the letter I asked my father to take good care of my two sisters and not allow strangers to stay in our home. Élise asked Aunt Monique, 'How are we going to get the letter to Jack?'

"'Don't worry about that,' Aunty said. 'We'll get someone he doesn't know to deliver the letter. He'll never guess that Lisa is staying with you.' I kissed Aunty, picked up my bag, and Élise and I left the house.

"Cousin Élise gave me a room in the attic of her house. 'Lisa,' she said, 'be careful. I don't want any of the neighbours finding out you live here. Don't go into the yard or the field. Just stay upstairs until we find a place for you to live.'

"Most of the time I stayed in the room, and occasionally Élise would come up and talk to me. At night when we were sure that no one would be visiting, I'd come downstairs and be with Élise and her husband. Every other day Aunt Monique would come to the house to check on me. One day she told me that she'd written a letter to her cousin Céline Miller in Montreal, asking if I could stay with her. Mrs. Miller was a very wealthy woman, she told me.

"I stayed almost three weeks with Élise, and then one day Aunt Monique came to give me the news. 'Listen, Lisa, Mrs. Miller is a cousin of mine, but her style of living is completely different from the way we live. She wants you to adapt to her environment, and she also wants you to forget about the Gaspé and your past. Are you ready to do that?'

"Worriedly I asked, 'You mean I can't write to you or have any information about you?'

"Aunty kissed me and said, 'Of course you can write to us. But you have to change your style of living.' I promised Aunty that I would do whatever Mrs. Miller wanted me to do.

"The next day Élise and I took the train to Montreal. It was my first trip out of my village, and I was nervous. Élise tried to calm me down, but I couldn't help it; after all, the trip to Montreal would change my life completely. I asked

Élise many questions, and she answered me as soothingly as possible. Once I asked, 'Do you think Mrs. Miller will like me?' and Élise said, 'Why not? She's our blood relative. Just because she married a rich man doesn't mean she'll forget her relatives. When your mother passed away, Mrs. Miller wrote a condolence letter to each of us. I haven't seen her for ages, but I'm sure she'll be delighted to see us.'"

Noel took me in his arms and kissed me. "Lisa, my love, I believe anyone who saw you would like you immediately. Why did you think Mrs. Miller wouldn't love you?"

"I don't know, but she was the only one who could release me from the hell I was living in. Please, Noel, just listen. We arrived in Montreal early in the morning. The crowds, the buildings and the traffic made me so disoriented that I was afraid I would fall; I grabbed Élise's hand tightly. 'It's okay, dear,' she assured me. 'Everything will be okay.' And with the address in her hand, we took a taxi to Mrs. Miller's house.

"Although to me it wasn't a house, it was a palace. A friendly housekeeper guided us to a large room and said, 'Please take a seat. Mrs. Miller will be with you shortly.' I was looking at the paintings on the wall when a slender elegant woman with the most alert eyes entered the room. She was very tall, and her high heels made her even taller. She looked at me and with a pleasant smile said, 'You must be Lisa. You're so lovely; you look like your mother, Marie-Josée.' All my nervousness vanished, and I felt I liked this tall woman. She came closer, and kissed Élise and me. Then she led us to the dining room for breakfast. Somehow I managed to eat without making too many mistakes. After breakfast Mrs. Miller took me upstairs and showed me my room. It was large and beautifully decorated. I rushed downstairs to bring up my bag, but Mrs. Miller stopped me and said, 'Listen, dear, forget about your bag and your things. In the afternoon two women will come by and make you some nice new clothes.' I just nodded my head.

"The next day cousin Élise headed back home despite Mrs. Miller wanting her to stay longer. In the late afternoon, as Élise was leaving, she kissed me and said, 'Lisa, I'm so happy for you. You're so lucky to live with our cousin. Be a good girl and don't worry about anything, especially about your sisters. Your aunt Monique and I will keep an eye on them.'

"With Élise gone I felt all alone in that huge house, and rushed to my room. Mrs. Miller had noticed my feelings; she came to my room and began to talk to me. 'My dear, you don't have to feel alone. I'm here for you. I want you to call me Aunty. After all, you're my blood; your mother was my dear cousin and I loved her a lot. Although she was much younger than me, we were close.'

"The more Mrs. Miller talked about my mother, the more I liked her.

"It took me almost a month to learn about my surroundings and also how to behave, how to talk, and all the other things I needed to know. One day when I was tired of all the training and reacted badly, Mrs. Miller sat down beside me, caressed my hair and said, 'Listen, Lisa my dear. I was born in the same village that you were born in and I was brought up there until I was eighteen. One day a wealthy man from Montreal came to our village about some kind of investment. He saw me working in the fields, he fell in love with me, and after we got married he brought me into this huge house with its servants. Do you think it was easy for me to learn all the things you're learning now?'

I looked into those beautiful, kind and alert eyes and said sharply, 'What's wrong with the way people live in our village? Actually I love the way we live there: we have freedom to eat, to talk, to wear what we want and to be in magnificent nature.'

"She smiled and said, 'Dear, nothing's wrong with the way you and I used to live, but each society has its own way of living. Since we're associating with different people, we have to act like them. Believe it or not, sometimes I have nostalgia for my past.'

"It was enough to convince me to listen and learn how to behave and act the way she wanted me to do in order to be acceptable to the people she mixed with.

"Mrs. Miller wanted me to call her by her first name, and I began calling her Aunty Céline. Gradually I grew closer to her, and eventually came to love her; I could see the love for me in her beautiful grey eyes too.

"She found a private school for me and enrolled me there. But for some reason she didn't want me going to school right away. She told the administration that I was out of town and would be back soon. Aunty was very interested in my hobbies. Many times she asked me about my pastimes. Finally I told her about my writings. She wanted to read whatever I wrote. I let her see some of the letters I'd written to my imaginary friend after the death of my mother, when I felt so lonesome. She couldn't believe that I'd done all those letters; she wanted to read more of my writings, so I gave her two of my poems to read. She was so moved by them that she called me into her room. 'My dear, you have such talent,' she said. 'You're really an artist. Besides your schoolwork, you'll have to work on your writings. And I'll help you in any way I can.'

"The next day at breakfast my aunty announced that she was throwing a big party and inviting all her friends in honour of me. I was panic-stricken. 'Aunty, you know how shy I am with people I've never met. And what will I wear?'

"'I don't want to hear any more of that kind of talk from you. You're a beautiful, brave and intelligent girl; you must take pride in yourself the same way I take pride in you. It will be an honour for my guests to meet you. And please don't worry about your dress; the dressmaker will make you the most beautiful gown.' I couldn't believe what I was hearing, but somehow I felt really good about myself.

"For more than a week everybody was busy with the big party, but Aunty asked me not to get involved and to remain calm, stay in my room and concentrate on my writings. But I couldn't help myself and now and then would go downstairs and have a look around. At one point, besides the two housekeepers I saw two young men decorating the dining table, arranging flowers and helping the cook. All these things made me tense and edgy. Anytime Aunty Céline saw me downstairs looking around perplexed, she would ask me to go back up. The day before the big party, she came to my room with the dressmaker. She was carrying a purple gown and asked me to try it on. I went into the corridor, where there was a full-length mirror, put the dress on and looked at myself: I couldn't believe that the girl in the mirror was me. When I went back into my room, my aunty couldn't help herself: she jumped up, took me in her arms and kissed me. 'Lisa, you look absolutely gorgeous, you look like a princess. Of course – you're my little princess!'

"The dressmaker said the gown was perfect, that she didn't need to make any adjustments. When she'd gone, Aunty Céline sat beside me and began to teach me how to behave at the party. 'Don't offer your hand to any of our guests unless they offer you their hand first,' she instructed. 'Then, as you shake the hand of that person, politely bow your head at the same time. Say nothing to people unless someone speaks to you or asks you a question. And try to always have the same opinion they have.'

"Impatiently I said, 'What else do I have to do?'

"'After you're dressed, you'll stay in your room until someone calls you, and then gracefully make your way down the stairway. I'll introduce you to my friends, and after dinner I'll ask you to read one of your poems.'

"'No way!" I exclaimed angrily. 'I'm not going to read my poem for a bunch of strangers!'

"Aunty said, 'You don't have to read one of your personal poems, just read the one about spring; it's about the beauty of nature and the revival of the earth. You can begin rehearsing your poem and you can also practice going up and coming down the staircase very graciously. Remember, when you come down the stairs hold on to the railing lightly, just to be safe.'

"The whole conversation and the preparations were ridiculous to me. At that moment I wished I were in my village in my little room and free of all these artificial things. But right away I thought of Rita and the life I'd been living, and decided to do whatever Aunty asked me to.

"Finally, at seven o'clock Saturday evening the doorbell began to ring and didn't stop. I sat in my gown in my room, until the housekeeper knocked on the door. 'It's time, Lisa,' she said.

"I looked once more in the mirror. Everything was perfect. I started down the stairs and saw almost a hundred people gathered in the hallway, almost all of them gazing up at me. I was so glad that Aunty had advised me to hold on to the railing; otherwise, I thought, I'd be rolling down instead of walking. I stopped on the last stair, as she'd directed me to, and Aunty Céline announced, 'My friends, I am proud to introduce my second cousin Lisa. Her parents wanted her to study in Europe, but since she's perfectly bilingual, they didn't know whether to send her to England or to France. I suggested Montreal, and I'm happy she chose to stay with me.'

"I joined the crowd and most of the guests shook my hand and said something nice to me, and as I'd been instructed, I replied with a polite sentence.

"After dinner Aunty asked me to read my poem. This was the part of the evening I'd least looked forward to, but I thought, 'Since I have to do this part of the play also, I may as well do it perfectly.' And I recited my poem with so much emotion that people applauded for a long time, and many of them came over to kiss me and congratulate me.

"When the party was over and everyone had gone I felt angry, sad and tired. I rushed upstairs to my room to change my clothes and go to bed. I heard a knock at the door; it was one of the housekeepers. 'Excuse me, Lisa, but Mrs. Miller wants to see you in the living room. Please don't change your clothes.' I was so annoyed with all the pretence that I didn't feel like having any conversation with Aunty Céline, but I didn't want to disobey the woman who was being so nice to me in her own way.

"Aunty Céline seemed satisfied with how the party had gone.

"'Come here, my dear. Come sit beside me, but first, please look at yourself in the mirror again. Your self-esteem must be very high tonight; you must be very proud of yourself.'

"As always, she was quick to notice my mood. 'What's the matter, dear. Didn't you like the party?'

"I couldn't keep it inside me. 'To be honest with you, Aunty, I feel bad about all those lies and that dishonesty.'

"She looked at me with those beautiful alert eyes and said, 'Dear, you'll soon learn that these people don't like to hear the truth, they all live in an artificial world. They're not sincere to each other, and everything is superficial.'

"'I felt tonight as though I was playing a part in one of the books I've read.'

"'Exactly! These people, when they get together, they all act.'

"'Then what was the point of tonight's party and all that work?'

"'On Monday, when you go to school for the first time, you'll find out. Now get a good night's sleep.'"

Noel broke into loud laughter. "What a lucky girl! When I was working so hard in Montreal and making deliveries on a rusty old bicycle, Mademoiselle Lisa was living like a princess in a castle." He leaned over and kissed me.

"You're wrong, Noel. The whole time I felt homesick for my birthplace," I said emotionally. "I felt I'd been thrown from my nest."

"We all have to be born somewhere," Noel said. "So what?"

That was enough to make me really angry. "When we were on the train, you were the one talking about the Gaspé and how beautiful it is, and about how you didn't want to go to Montreal. Now you're blaming me for missing my birthplace when I was just a teenager."

"Hold on. This is completely different. You were living in a dream world and yet you were unhappy and thinking about the past. Besides, there was no home for you in the Gaspé. You had decided to leave yourself."

"I was a teenager, emotionally disturbed, when I arrived in that huge house to begin living with a stranger."

"But she wasn't a stranger. The way you talk about her, it seems to me that she was a wonderful woman."

"It's true she was a marvellous person. I was the one who had problems. I couldn't free myself from my mother's death, from Rita and how ruthless she'd been and above all from Chris and what he'd done to me."

Noel stroked my hair. "I'm sorry, dear. Please tell me the rest."

I took a deep breath and begun to talk again. I really wanted to be finished with my story.

"On Monday, when I went to the private school that Aunty had enrolled me in, to my surprise I didn't feel I was a stranger. It seemed as though most of the kids knew me already, and some of them appeared eager to be friends with me. I didn't understand the reason, until a charming girl came up to me and said, 'So you're the poet. My mother told me all about you.' And I realized that all the hard work and the big party that Aunty had arranged were all for me: she didn't want the kids at school to look at me like a stranger but as an equal. She didn't want me to have to explain to the kids who I was. That was wonderful, because I had worried that the other students would look down on me.

"In the afternoon, as soon as I arrived home I rushed to kiss my aunty and thank her for all the hard work she'd done for me. Aunty looked at me intently and said, 'Now you know how to deal with these people. And remember, no matter how close you get to your friends, never ever talk about your past.'

Noel seemed to be enjoying my story. "There you are. Who would have expected that the party would lead to that? As I said before, you were a lucky girl." I didn't answer. I wasn't anxious to have disagreements with Noel. I just wanted to get through telling him my story.

"Things were looking okay in Aunt Céline's house, and we became close. One Sunday afternoon as we were having tea she told me more about herself and about her relationship with her late husband, and how much she'd loved him. 'I had a son,' she confided. 'If he were alive today, he'd be twenty-five years old.'

"Her face covered over with gloom, and finally she managed to tell me about how, seven years earlier, her husband and her son had gone sailing with a friend, their boat had turned over, and they'd drowned."

"Poor Aunty," Noel said. For a while we sat in silence.

"Listen, the rain has stopped. Would you like to go for a walk in the fresh air?"

I wasn't in the mood to go out, but Noel insisted. "Let's put your aunt and her personal tragedy aside for a while." I put my coat on, and as we were going out, Francine called after me, "Where are you going with those shoes?" She handed me her rain boots, and they fitted me perfectly; I kissed her and we ran out.

Noel put his arm around my waist as we walked on the wet ground. It was messy walking, but we didn't care, we were just careful where we stepped. We ended up in the forest, at the same place where we'd made love the first time. Noel wanted to make love to me again. I looked at him and begun to laugh. "Are you crazy? Everything's wet: the ground, the leaves. We'll be soaking!"

He smiled. "Yes, I know. I want you to enjoy this moment of life. Even walking in this weather is one of life's joys. When you were telling me the story of your aunt, in the beginning I thought, what a lucky woman she was, so rich, she had everything; but when you told me about the accident I realized that death treats us equally, that life is just a moment and you have to take advantage of each moment in that moment. The story of your mother, my time with Isabel, your aunt's young son and her husband all teach us that we have to hold on to every moment in life." He kissed me intensely. We lay on the wet leaves and enjoyed the moment of being one.

On the way back it began to pour really hard, and when we arrived at Francine's we were soaking wet. It took us some time to dry off. At the dinner table, Francine looked at us with a caring smile and said, "I've never seen people so crazy in love as you."

I was getting ready for bed when Noel took my hand gently and said, "You haven't finished. I want to know what happened after Aunty told you about the tragedy in her life and I want to know the most important part of yours: when did you fall in love and who was that person?" We lay on the bed and I went on with my story.

"My relationship with Aunt Céline took a different direction that day. After what she'd told me, for a few days I felt terribly guilty for judging her to be an artificial woman. At night when I was alone I thought of her and said to myself, 'Poor Aunty. She's suffered more than I did, yet she pretends to live the way people around her want her to live.' We grew closer and understood each other better. First

thing in the morning I would run to see her and in the afternoon when I came back from school I would do the same.
When I didn't find her in the living room, worriedly I
would search the house and ask the housekeepers, 'Where
is she? Where is she?' And Aunty would do the same thing;
if she had a lunch meeting or other engagement she would
try to be home when I got back from school. She became
the mother I'd lost and I became the child that had vanished from her life. Living with Aunty was quiet and pleasant. The more I learned about her personality and her
compassion, the more I loved her. After the death of her
family, she had involved herself actively with many charita-
ble organizations and donated almost half the wealth she'd
inherited from her husband to them. Also, she gave money
to universities for scholarship funds."

Noel said, "What bad judgment. In the beginning you
had a totally wrong impression of your aunt."

I got annoyed. "Are you trying to find flaws in my
character? I told you before, at that time I was a teenager
with a bunch of chips on my shoulder."

Noel right away corrected himself. "I meant to say, try
not to misjudge *me*. I love you beyond your imaginings.
That was all I meant. Please go on."

"I traveled with my aunty to many places in the world.
We went to Europe, to North Africa, South America. In
the winter, during the holidays we would visit one of the
Caribbean islands.

"All those years I never forgot my sisters, my Aunt Monique and my father. Since from the very beginning after I
came to Montreal Aunty didn't want me to have any direct
communication with my family, she would write to Aunt
Monique herself that I was doing fine. I would occasionally

send gifts to my sisters through a third party. I didn't know what the arrangement was, but I knew that my sisters and father did not know where I was living.

"Aunty Céline encouraged me to work on my poems as well as on my other writings. When I was in college my poems appeared in several literary magazines. And shortly after I graduated my first collection was published. I knew Aunty had some influence in the publication of my book, but she was so happy and proud of my achievement.

"Aunty was getting older, and since she wasn't socializing as much as before, she decided to sell the house. She bought a smaller place in the same area, and she also bought a nice house for me. 'This is your security,' she said. 'You rent out the house and put the money in the bank. Since you live with me, you don't need to touch the income.' And the money collected in the bank for my future.

"We would still go traveling in the summertime."

Noel smiled. "I'd love to travel with you and see the world."

"Please, Noel," I said. "Let me finish the story. I want to get it over with and sleep.

"I was studying literature at university and I loved my courses. It was the winter holiday and Aunty and I decided to go to Egypt. I'd always been fascinated by the rich culture and great civilization of that country. We'd traveled once before to Egypt and enjoyed our visit, so we decided to go back. It was on that trip that my whole life changed. We were staying in a beautiful hotel and we had a panoramic view of the Nile from our rooms. One day after we came back from a tour of the Pyramids and had our lunch in the hotel restaurant, Aunty went up to her room for a nap. I didn't feel like sleeping, so I headed to the small café in the hotel for an espresso. I was passing through the lobby when someone caught my eye in the tiny office behind the information desk. A handsome, distinguished-looking young Egyptian man was sitting comfortably on an antique chair, gazing back at me. Suddenly I felt the ground was shaking. As I stood there unable to move, the young man came out of the office and walked towards me."

"'Hello,' he said. 'My name is Simon. May I offer you a cup of coffee?' I nodded dumbly, and we walked over to the hotel café.

"How long we stayed there I don't know. We talked and talked. He told me he was the eldest son of the owner of the hotel, that the family were Copts, and that he'd studied engineering in the United States but his father wanted him to come back to Egypt and run the hotel."

I looked at Noel as I talked for his reaction, and could read jealousy on his face. He tried to sound indifferent to the subject of Simon, but wasn't very successful. "You didn't tell me how he looked? Was he handsome?"

"Do you really want to know?" I asked.

"Of course I want to know," he said sharply; "I want to picture him in my mind."

"He was the most handsome creature in this world. He looked like the Greek heroes of the epic poems."

"Have you ever seen one of those heroes?"

"No, but I can picture them."

"You have a powerful imagination," Noel said petulantly. "I can't."

"He had the most beautiful black velvet eyes, with thick eyebrows that gave his eyes even more depth. He was tall, with a strong slim body, short black curly hair and olive skin. And he had the most exceptional manners."

"Well I'm the complete opposite of him," said Noel, "since I have no black velvet eyes, and therefore you can't be in love with me."

"Stop being silly," I said. "To make a long story shorter, I was so in love with him that I didn't want to leave Egypt. I had the chance to meet his family, and he wanted to marry me right away. Aunty was totally opposed, and asked me to go back with her to Montreal and think it over, and I did, but I knew what I wanted. After a couple of months Simon traveled to Montreal and asked me to return with him to Egypt and marry him there, and I accepted. Aunty did not come with me to Egypt for the wedding. When I was about to leave Montreal, she called me to her room and said unhappily, 'I know you won't listen to me and you'll do whatever you want to do, but I feel I have to tell you what I think. I hope I'm wrong,' she said, taking my hand and looking directly into my eyes. 'You're leaving your education and your country for a man you don't know very well. You're going off to live in a country where the culture and language are different. Think twice before you go, and let me tell you something else. There's no home for you here if God forbid things go wrong and you come back. You'll be on your own. You can come visit me, but not live with me. This is not a threat, these are the facts.' All these years later I still have the sound in my ears of what Aunty said to me that day.

"We had a luxurious wedding in Egypt. Simon was my whole life and I was so happy. We lived in his parents' house, a mansion. There was an inner courtyard, and all the rooms were arranged around it. The windows opened onto the courtyard, from which there was no connection to the outside word. Simon's father was king of that palace.

"Simon would go to work early in the morning and come back home late in the evening, and I could go nowhere alone. All this seemed okay to me as long as I had Simon, but gradually things changed – especially when Simon's parents found out that I couldn't have children. I'd had surgery to seal my tubes. I told Simon that because of how my mother died I never ever wanted to have children."

Noel looked at me in surprise. "Really? Is that true? You went through surgery in order not to have any children?"

"Yes, Noel. The day I saw my mother soaked in her blood I made a pledge to myself that I would never give birth to a child.

"In time, life in Simon's father's house became uneasy for me, and as an individual I felt I had no freedom. My living conditions made me ask myself if I had any right to personal happiness, and I had the terrible feeling all the time of belonging to someone other than myself. His father looked at his wife the way one looks at a valuable piece of personal property. In that crowded house even the wind had no freedom; there was no air to breathe and I felt suffocated. But still I tolerated the situation because of the love I had for Simon. I knew he loved me too, but his father had considerable power over him and Simon had to listen to whatever his father had to say. Gradually our relationship turned in a different direction. He would spend more of his time in the hotel and sometimes would go out at night with his friends. I was left alone most of the time, but I kept myself busy with my writing.

"One evening when I was working at my desk, one of the servants came to my room. She sat down close to me and asked me to listen to her. I was surprised: in that house the servants were not allowed to come to your room unless you called them, and usually they would stay at the door; yet this one not only came into my room, she locked the door too. At first I was alarmed, but she asked me to be quiet. She begged me not to say a word to anyone, and I promised her. She told me that when Simon was studying in the U.S., he'd married an American woman and had had a son from that marriage, and when he came back to Egypt he'd divorced his American wife, and the son was living with the mother back in the States. Except now they were in Egypt for a visit, and Simon's father was planning to hire her to work in the hotel, and Simon was going off to see them every night. The servant told me all the details and left the room. For a moment I felt as though someone had grabbed me by the head and smacked it against the wall. My head was spinning, but I pulled myself together and realized there was no point in confronting Simon. I decided simply to leave him.

"I packed some belongings and in the dark of night, exactly the way I'd run off from my father's home, I left the house and went straight to the airport. Luckily there was a flight to Canada that night. By midnight, exactly the time Simon would be coming home, I was on an aircraft flying over Cairo and leaving the man I'd loved. At that moment I realized that nothing is more important in our lives than our freedom."

I looked at Noel lovingly. "And that's the story of my life," I said simply.

Noel answered, "It's not finished; tell me what happened after."

"It's obvious. I moved to the house that Aunty bought for me earlier, got my divorce and devoted my life to my writings. I published a few novels and another poetry collection. I've lived alone, and will never be married again. Not ever."

Noel asked, "What about your aunt?"

"Once or twice a week I would go and see her. She never blamed me for my mistakes."

"Did you suffer a lot after you left Egypt?"

"Not really. I made a big mistake and I learned from it. Besides, I suffered more during the time I was living in the house of Simon's father."

"How long ago did that whole business take place, and what finally happened to your aunt."

"It's more than a decade since I got my divorce. My aunty, she passed away just last year and her death had a huge impact on me. Again I felt that part of my life was lost. This is my first trip to the Gaspé since her death. Don't forget, she didn't want me to remember my past or to visit my birthplace. That was the first condition I had to accept when I moved into her house, and I respected her wishes until her death."

And with that I said good-night to Noel and finally got to sleep.

The next morning after breakfast, Noel and I left the house for our walk; he was very quiet and reserved. When we arrived at our special place in the forest and sat down on the mound of dry leaves, he began to talk.

"I was very touched by your story. Though I felt that you left out a lot of it, especially about your relationship with Simon. Also that you tried to avoid talking about your time of grief and the period when you blamed yourself, but I'm so sorry you had to pay such a heavy price for your mistake. Did you ever admit to yourself that it was poor judgment, and do you think that you learned from it?"

"What's the point of talking about it now? Besides, we're all the victims of our shortcomings, but we also learn from our mistakes. That was a chapter of my life, and now it's closed."

"But it's *not* over; the experience you had with Simon has an effect on your life."

"I don't really know what you're talking about. What are you trying to say?"

Noel took my hand and looked directly into my eyes. "I meant that I want to marry you, and I'm not like Simon. I'm Noel, who is passionately in love with you."

I couldn't believe it. I took my hand away from his, got up off the ground and said to him, "I'm sorry if I gave you the impression that I'll marry you. How did that idea ever enter your mind in the first place?"

Noel's face grew pale. I felt bad for him. I sat back down beside him and gently said, "My love, why did you think we should get married?"

Noel had got his nerve back, and replied, "I love you. Love is the greatest emotion in our lives, and we have a right to love and be loved."

"Love is an imperfect approximation of closeness," I said, and smiled.

"Don't say these silly things that you don't believe yourself."

"Listen, dear Noel," I said as tenderly as possible. The last thing I wanted was to hurt his feelings. "When you're in love, you always close your eyes to reality and you always begin by deceiving yourself, and ultimately will end up deceiving others. First there's a passionate, fascinating love affair, and then in no time at all we'll end up hurting each other."

"Is that your definition of love and togetherness, and also your explanation for living alone in this world?"

"As I told you before, Noel, life is a road that you travel alone. And you have to learn to be good company for yourself."

The expression on Noel's face was changing and he was growing more agitated. He frowned and said, "You mean it's not a normal thing for two people who love each other to get married?"

"We've known each other for less than two weeks. Besides, we don't have a normal life; we're artists. You're a painter and I'm a writer."

"But do we not have a right to get married and live a normal life?"

"I'm afraid the answer's no. Getting married means limiting yourself. An artist must always live alone. We're already married – to our art."

"I'd rather have you in my life than my art," Noel answered angrily.

"But my world is my art, and I know that painting is *your* world," I said sharply. "For me it's the only life that makes me happy. Without my art I'm nothing."

Our conversation was turning into an argument. So I said, "Let's go on with our walk; we can continue our discussion later on."

But Noel didn't want to end our talk. "No," he said. "I want to know more about your reasons."

Calmly and without looking at him I said, "If you have a powerful imaginative life, your personal life becomes more colourless."

"But sometimes reality is more powerful than the imagination."

"Just for a short while."

Noel raised his voiced angrily. "I don't understand you. You made love to me, you told me that you love me, you told me the whole story of your life and you've lived with me for more than a week under one roof and now you're telling me that you want to go on with your life and leave me alone."

"You told me before that the moment you saw me you fell in love with me; so that wasn't my fault. Besides, loving each other has nothing to do with marriage."

"First tell me, Lisa: do you really love me?"

"You know very well how much I care for you."

"So what is this nonsense? Why don't you want to marry me?"

"Noel think about it, dear. After we got married, you would be a river and I would be just the banks of that river. I don't want that. I want to be a river myself and flow until I join the ocean."

"We can both be a river."

"And where will the banks be?" I asked. Noel had grown dejected by our conversation. He gazed at me deeply and with a sad voice said, "You're making the biggest mistake imaginable. You'll end up living alone for the rest of your life."

"The bird that soars beyond its own boundaries must have strong wings and powerful determination, and I have that."

"If you're telling me you don't want to marry me," Noel said angrily, "then our relationship is over."

"Not necessarily. We can still see each other."

"No, Lisa. I want to marry you, to live with you. I want to have you always beside me. In the morning when I open my eyes I want to see your beautiful face, and at night I want your haunting eyes to be the last thing I see before I go to sleep. I don't want to live the way you want to live."

Noel got up. I got up too, and without saying another word to each other we walked off.

Noel decided to leave Francine's house; he wanted to continue his trip to the Gaspé without me. The whole evening he didn't say a word to me and at breakfast he was quiet too. He looked devastated, but he didn't want to admit it. He ignored me completely, saying only, "One of us will get on this train, either you or me. I can stay here and take the next train, if you want to go now."

"No. You go today. I'll stay with Francine a couple more days."

The morning Noel left, he was angry and teary-eyed. Bitterly he said, "I felt that we were going to be inseparable, forever. Who would have expected it to end like this? What you've done to me I'm sure you'll regret for the rest of your life."

* * *

So many years after that journey to the Gaspé, the memories were still fresh in my mind. It was on that trip that I'd met Noel. He was a handsome young painter who wanted to revisit his birthplace too. We fell in love, we got off the train, we stayed in a small village together, and we separated. But the week we spent together was the most memorable time of my life.

He decided to leave me when he found out I wasn't going to marry him. The instant he walked off to catch the train I regretted letting him go; I speedily packed my things and raced after him, but it was too late, the train had gone by the time I reached the station.

I left my bag there and walked to the forest, to the place we'd used to go together, the place where he'd made love to me for the first time. I threw myself down on the dry leaves at the foot of a naked maple tree and began to weep.

I took the next day's train to the Gaspé; I couldn't stay any longer in the room where we'd spent more than a week together and shared our lives as one.

I was hoping I could find him in the Gaspé, but it was a false hope. I filled my time getting to know my family again. My sisters, in their early twenties now, were both newly married and planning families of their own. My father was still married to Rita; seeing her brought back memories of the unhappiness she and her brother had caused me. I felt I no longer belonged in my village, and after a short time I left to go back to Montreal. I had strong hopes of finding Noel there. I hadn't changed my views on marriage, but I still wanted to be with him. In the brief period of time we'd spent together, he'd become part of me.

As the days turned to weeks, months and years, I never stopped thinking of Noel. He had vanished from my life, but the sweet memories of him and the image of his face kept coming back to me, and I could not be free of him. I felt so empty without him; all I wanted to do was escape from myself. I determined to leave Montreal and travel to Africa. I thought the wonders of the landscape and wildlife and the rich ancient civilizations might bring me peace. I rented out the house that my aunty bought for me long before and set off on my journey.

I'd visited various countries in East Africa; I'd traveled to Ethiopia, Sudan, Tanzania and Kenya. But I'd fallen in love with Kenya and its beauty, especially after visiting its national parks. I wanted to live in a small village in an agricultural region, and I was able to find a nice clean house in the central highlands that could be rented inexpensively. The natural beauty surrounding me gave me energy and inspired me to devote my life to my writings, and the kindness of the people in the village encouraged me to help them in any way I could. But Noel was never out of my thoughts. Despite the fulfilment I achieved in my work and the pleasures of travel and meeting new people, there was an emptiness inside me that nothing or no one else could fill.

In the early morning I would go for my walk and enjoy the magnificent views. On one of those mornings I met up with a young woman rushing along the narrow path. As she pushed past me she said, "Sorry, I am late for school."

Surprised, I asked, "Where *is* the school?"

She smiled. "I can't give you any address, so if you want to know where the school is, you have to come with me." And I walked along with her. She was a beautiful woman, with the most enthralling eyes. From the way she dressed, you could see that she was from the town. Without my asking, she said, "My name is Sabrina, and I am the only teacher for the children of this village." After I introduced myself I said, "If you need any help, I'll be happy to do what I can." She stopped walking, put her arms around me and kissed me on the forehead. "Thank you. *Thank you.* I need help desperately. But let's go faster, the children are waiting for me."

We came to a small field with a hut sitting in the middle of it. The children's mothers stood around outside, looking down the path for Sabrina. When we arrived the mothers left, and I entered the hut with Sabrina to find about fifteen very young pupils seated on benches.

Sabrina talked in Swahili, and I knew only a few words. "Don't worry," she said to me, "we will speak in English after an hour." Before too long Sabrina asked if I would get up and help her. It was the beginning of a regular job for me. Each day began very early, since the children's mothers had to get to work in the fields soon after sunup.

Sabrina and I became good friends as well as a teaching team. The children we were working with were actually preschoolers, between three and five. There was a little girl that I loved a lot; to me she was the child that I could never have. From time to time with the permission of her mother I would take her to my little house and work with her, and then deliver her to her mother in the evening. Gradually she didn't want to go home anymore, and spent much of the time with me. Her charming character and her affection for me inspired me to write a story about the children of the village that became a very successful book throughout East Africa.

Often at night Sabrina would come to my home, and after dinner we would talk about the next day's project for our kids. I became involved in a great many projects along with my writings, and my life no longer felt dull. Life had meaning and I was enjoying it, but still I could not free myself from Noel and all those wonderful memories.

On one of the nights Sabrina came for dinner she told me that when she was a student in London she'd fallen in love with one of her classmates. They got married, and they both took employment as social workers for the government. But after a couple of years of marriage she got divorced and came back to her native land to help the children and women there. Sabrina didn't go into the details of her life, nor did she mention why her marriage broke up.

When she finished, I told her about my love for Noel, which I carried still. Out of nowhere Sabrina grew outraged and began to shout, "To hell with him! Forget about him! Men do not deserve our love."

I was astounded at her reaction. "Why are you talking that way? Did I say something to upset you?"

"Of course. You made me angry when you said that you miss Noel. To hell with him. To hell with all of them!"

She picked up her cup and made as though to drink some tea. I remained quiet and gazed down into my cup, but I could hear the tears in Sabrina's voice as she began to talk.

"In spite of the disapproval of my parents, I got married to a bloody man. You have no idea what he did to me. He took off with my best friend; you don't know the pain that I went through. Now all I feel is anger inside me."

I tried to calm her down. As gently as I could I said, "Not all men are the same. My Noel was wonderful – it was me who left *him*. I know I hurt him badly, and I regret it."

Sabrina looked at me the way you look at a naive child. "They are all the same. Don't be fooled by the beautiful words they whisper in your ears. After a while, they get tired of your bed and they look for a new one."

I was going to say something but Sabrina cut me off. "Listen, Lisa, you can't change my opinion about men. And if you want to be so romantic and spend the rest of your life thinking of Noel, then be my guest." I realized Sabrina was so bitter that no one could have a useful discussion with her. And I never brought Noel's name up in front of Sabrina again. But I felt so sorry for her, for what had happened to her in her early life that had turned her into a woman with so much hate and anger.

But Sabrina and I worked beautifully together, and our usefulness to the village community made us happy. The years passed peacefully by, until one day I received a letter from my tenant saying that they were planning to move to Vancouver. Although my real-estate agent could have managed to rent the house again, I decided to go back home and arrange things myself – and maybe take up my search for Noel once more. I talked to Sabrina. She agreed, but said, "Don't leave me alone for more than a month."

In Montreal I stayed with Sylvia, one of my old friends from university. I spent my time visiting places I'd used to go to with my aunt, making side trips to stop in front of the house we'd shared, the schools I'd attended – and occasionally dropping in to art galleries in the hope of finding a painting by Noel. At night I would share my adventures with Sylvia, but I never told her about my quest.

One day Sylvia asked me to go to a gallery with her; she said there was an exhibit by a wonderful painter named Noel. I couldn't believe what I'd heard. I asked for the name of the artist again. "His name is Noel. He's from the Gaspé. He lives there and never leaves the area. He's becoming very well known."

For two days I fidgeted. I couldn't sleep at night. I hadn't told my friend anything about my past relationship with Noel. The day before the exhibit there was an article about him with his picture in the newspaper. Impatiently I read it, and then sat up late into the night looking at his picture. Noel had changed a lot. His hair had some grey in it, like mine, and his face had become more distinguished with age.

I couldn't believe how many people were at the gallery. There was a buzz in the air. Everybody was talking about

Noel, and people were snatching up his paintings.

In one corner of the gallery a few paintings had been hung under a "Not for sale" sign. I looked carefully. One was the portrait of me he had drawn when we stayed in Francine's house. There was a title under the painting: "FIND HER FOR ME." Another was of the woods where we used to walk, and there was also a beautiful drawing of Francine's house. I trembled as I stood looking at those works. Suddenly I felt a woman at my side. Regarding me closely, she said, "Could that possibly be your portrait?"

All those years that I'd been searching for Noel, he'd stayed in the Gaspé hoping I would find him. I got his address from the gallery, and the next day I took the train for the Gaspé to see my love. The whole trip I could feel myself shaking nervously. It was impossible to stay in my seat; I paced back and forth, from one car to the other, wondering how he would react when he saw me, how *I* would react when I saw *him*.

I thought, when I see him, the first thing I'll say is, "Noel, would it be too late if I asked you to marry me?"

But I never got the chance to ask him. The next morning, when I arrived in the Gaspé, mourners had gathered to bury my love, Noel.

Autumn Bird

selected poems

Snow

Seven days,
Seven nights,
All week long
The white powder
Pouring down,
Pouring down.

The earth is white
And white,
Getting large
And large;
The earth is pregnant.

The earth is pregnant
Seven months,
But soon in the spring
The earth will deliver
Its children,
The colourful flowers.

I will pick some,
Then come to see you.

Bandage

Whenever I fell,
Whenever I was wounded,
Mother was there with a bandage.

In childhood
The pain was part of play;
The pain would disappear with the game.

Now the wounds of my soul
Do not disappear with any game or bandage.
They have become a part of my life,
And patiently I carry them
On my shoulder.

Autumn Bird

The autumn bird
Flies, flies far away;
Leaves me and everything behind.

I wish
I could fly far, far away;
Leave you and everything behind,
Like the autumn bird.

Backpack

We became two strangers
Side by side
Under one roof.

We could not stand
The air we breathed
Under one roof.

We were at the end
Of our road
Under one roof.

I packed my bag.
I walked and walked
On a new road.

Exhausted, I sat beside the road.
I opened my backpack,
And you were there.

Wind

All day,
All night
The fierce wind blows,
Taking all my belongings.

O wild wind,
Take everything you need,
Except the memories of my love.

Did Not Know

They cut my wings,
And no one taught me
How to fly.

Yet, when they opened
The door
Of my cage,

I flew, I flew,
I flew far, far away;
I flew far, far away,

So far that no one
Could put me
In the cage again.

My Name

Once I asked my mother,
Mother, what is the meaning of my name?

Star in the sky, my little girl.

Then what am I doing
Here on earth?

The Sky and I

Every fall
Out of sadness
Like the sky
I, too, cry
For the flowers that die.

Every spring
Out of joy
Like the sky
I, too, cry
For the flowers that sprout.

Newly Planted Trees

On the last day of fall
I kissed my twelve newly planted trees.

Good-bye, I said,
I will return in the spring.

They began to cry:
Don't leave us alone!
Don't leave us alone!

We are afraid of the rain,
Of the snow,
Of the wind,
Of the darkness.

They began to shout:
Don't leave us alone!
Don't leave us alone!

I caressed them and said,
Don't be afraid,
Don't be afraid.

You are children of the Gaspé;
You will survive,
You will survive.

Song for the Gaspé

I am a bird
Free of its cage in the Gaspé.

I am a child
Beginning to walk in the Gaspé.

I am a butterfly
On wild flowers in the Gaspé.

I am the flow
Of roaring rivers in the Gaspé.

I am the wind
Of the ocean in the Gaspé.

I am the guest
Of stars in the Gaspé.

I am the awakening
Of morning glories in the Gaspé.

I am the Gaspé
When I am in the Gaspé.

The Window

On a cold snowy day,
Hungry and frozen,
A little bird
Searching for shelter and food
Saw through the window of a grand house
A caged bird looking out.

The little bird peeked in the window;
Oh, you lucky caged bird!
You have everything:
You have warmth,
You have water,
You have food;
I do not.

The caged bird sighed
A cold sigh:
I wish I could
Fly like you.

Playmate

The best playmate
Of my childhood
Was my little sister,
With captivating azure eyes.

One day
On the shore
A huge wave
Devoured her.

She was
Only four
When she became
Four thousand years old.

Forty years later
On the same shore
A little girl
With the same captivating azure eyes
Came out from the sea,
Walked towards me and took my hand.

Sometimes

Sometimes I want to be a bird,
To fly.

Sometimes I want to be a fire,
To flame.

Sometimes I want to be a wind,
To blow.

Sometimes I want to be a cloud,
To rain.

Sometimes I want to be a star,
To shine.

Sometimes I want to be lightning,
To strike.

But most of the time
I want to be me;
To be me
To love you
For all these lost times.

Return

When the sun begins to flame again
When snow slakes the earth's thirst;
To the sound of opening leaves,
To the sound of saluting waves,
To the sound of chanting birds,
To the sound of dancing winds
I will return to you again,
O blue-green Gaspé.

For Mona

She is neither my mother nor my daughter;
She is neither my sister nor my aunt;
She is neither from my country nor
    my continent.

She is a daughter of Egypt,
Filled with treasure,
And generous as the Nile.

Like the Pyramids
She is formidable,
Yet tender as morning dew.

Beautiful as her soul,
Warm as her land,
And full of love.

In the tumbling of my soul
To the lonely depths of an abyss
She held my hand.

In the darkest time
Of my wounded body
She walked with me.

They call her Mona;
I call her ultimate human.

Why Birds Fly

Once a little girl asked
Why birds fly,
And I said:

Once there was a she-bird and a he-bird;
They built a house,
A beautiful one.

One day when they were not in,
An angry wind arrived,
And took the house.

From that time
All birds fly
To catch the wind.

They fly and fly
From sea to sea,
From mountain to mountain.

They fly from
Forest to forest,
From desert to desert.

To find the wind,
All birds
Fly and fly.

They fly to find the wind,
To find the house of the wind,
To get their house from the wind.

As they fly, they sing:
Where is the wind?
Where is the wind?

The Earth

O my friend.
When they gave you to the earth,
The earth had a mountain
Of snow on its shoulders.

I wonder now
Why like flowers
You don't sprout
In the spring.

Friends

When I was a child, the rain was my friend;
I would let the rain wash my hair.

When I was a child, the wind was my friend;
I would let the wind play with my hair.

When I was a child, the sun was my friend;
I would let the sun brighten my hair.

When I was a child, the sea was my friend;
I would let the sea caress my hair.

Now my lonely white hair
Has lost all her friends.

The Bells

Only three times
Do the bells toll for us.

The first,
When we get our name.

The second,
When we get the addition to our name.

The third,
When they wipe out our name.

Time

You were nowhere
In my childhood.

You lived in my city
In my youth.

You lived in my street
In my adult life.

You live now in my home
In my old years.

O death.

You Will Hear

After me, put my ashes
Under a small tree in my village.
The small tree will grow;
It will grow tall and green.

The leaves will grow big and green.
With every wind
You will hear the leaves
Reciting my poetry.

After me, put my ashes
Under a small tree in the Gaspé.
It will grow tall and green.

The birds will build their nests
In this tree.
They will sing songs
In this tree.

And every dawn
You will hear the birds
Twittering my poetry.

After me, put my ashes
Under a small tree in my village.
The small tree will grow;
It will grow tall and green.

And every spring
You will hear
The birds, the leaves, the wind,
The people of my village
All chanting my poetry.

Free Bird

Free bird,
Take me with you
Wherever you go.

I will fly with you
Over the crowded cities,
Over the silent valleys,
Over the fresh prairies.

Free bird,
Take me with you
Wherever you go.

I will soar with you
Over the immense skies,
Over the great oceans,
Over the majestic forests.

I will rise at dawn with you;
I will walk at sunset with you;
I will inhale the sweet air with you;
I will sing our song with you.

Free bird,
Take me with you
Wherever you go.

I will cleanse my wings
In the ocean's waves with you;
I will dance barefoot
On the heated shore with you.

Free bird,
Take me with you
Wherever you go.

I will fly with you,
I will fly with you,
I will fly with you,
Then soar into eternity.